The Dolphin Rider
and Other Greek Myths

Mary S. Sheros
P.O. Box 504
Alamosa, Co. 81101

by BERNARD EVSLIN

Illustrated by Jerry Contreras

SCHOLASTIC INC.
New York Toronto London Auckland Sydney

For Tanya
who listens with her eyes

ISBN 0-590-00128-0

12 11 10 9 8 7   6 7 8 9/8   0/9

Printed in the U.S.A.   11

Contents

The Dolphin Rider 1

The Gift of Fire 7

The Mysterious Box 13

Narcissus and Echo 19

Wild Horses of the Sun 29

The Solid Gold Princess 42

The Dragon's Teeth 49

The Beautiful Witch 77

Keeper of the Winds 94

Cupid and Psyche 111

The Man Who Overcame Death 125

Afterword 138

The Dolphin Rider

This is the tale of Arion. He was a very talented young man who asked Apollo, the god of music, to teach him the lyre. Apollo was so amused by this bold request, which no one in the world had dared to make before, that he taught Arion to play the lyre most beautifully.

Now Arion lived in a city near the sea called Corinth. He was a bold, adventure-loving youth, and wanted very much to travel. But when he was a child an oracle, foretelling the future, had said, "Avoid the sea. For no ship will bring you back from any voyage you make." Arion's parents believed this, and made him stay at home.

But the boy grew more restless every day. He would go down to the harbor and watch the ships scudding out to the open sea, their sails spread to the wind. When he saw this he felt full of longing for far places. He would unsling his lyre and sing a song of ships and storms and castaways...of giants and cannibals and sea-monsters, and all the adventures he had dreamed of.

His song was so beautiful that dolphins rose to the surface to listen. They sat there in the water, balancing themselves on their tails, listening. Sometimes they wept great salt tears. When Arion stopped singing, they clapped their flippers, shouting, "Bravo! Bravo! More...More!" and he would have to sing again. Often he sang to them all night long. And when the stars paled he could see giant shadows gliding nearby — swordfish and sharks, devilfish and giant turtles, which had risen from the depths, not for an easy meal, but to listen to the enchanting sounds he was making.   •

Then, for his twentieth birthday, Apollo gave Arion a golden lyre. The youth was eager to try it out at the great music festival held in Sicily.

"Oracles and soothsayers are gloomy by nature," he told himself. "How often do they tell you anything happy? They try to scare you so that you'll come back and pay them again, hoping to hear something better. Anyway, that's what I choose to believe, for I must see the world no matter what happens."

So Arion took his lyre and set sail for Sicily. He played and sang so beautifully in the festival that the audience went mad with delight. They heaped gifts upon him — a jeweled sword, a suit of silver armor, an ivory bow and quiver of bronze-tipped arrows, and a fat bag of gold. Arion was so happy that he forgot all about the prophecy. In his eagerness to get home and tell about his triumphs, he took the first ship back to Corinth, although the captain was a huge, ugly, dangerous-looking fellow, with an even uglier crew.

On the first afternoon out, Arion was sitting in the bow, gazing at the purple sea, when the captain strode up and said, "Pity — you're so young to die."

"Am I to die young?" Arion asked.

"Yes."

"Are you sure?"

"Absolutely certain."

"What makes you so sure?"

"Because I'm going to kill you."

"That does seem a pity," said Arion. "When is this sad event to take place?"

"Soon. In fact, immediately."

"But why? What have I done?"

"Something foolish. You let yourself become the owner of a treasure that I must have — that jewelled sword, the silver armor, not to mention that delicious, fat bag of gold. You should never show things like that to thieves."

"Why can't you take what you want without killing me?"

"Too big a risk, my boy. You might complain to the king about being robbed, and that would be very dangerous for us. So you have to go. I'm sure you understand."

"I see you've thought the matter over carefully," said Arion. "Well, I have only this to ask: Let me sing a last song before I die."

At the music festival, Arion had composed a song of praise to be sung on special occasions. And he sang it now — praising first Apollo, who had taught him music, then old Neptune, master of the sea. He sang praise to the sea itself and those who dwell there — the gulls and ocean nymphs and gliding fish. He sang to the magic changefulness of the waters, which put on different colors as the sun climbs and sinks.

So singing, Arion leaped from the bow of the ship, lyre in hand, and plunged into the sea.

He had sung so beautifully that the creatures of the deep had swum up to hear him. Among them was a school of dolphins. The largest one quickly dived, then rose to the surface, lifting Arion on his back.

"Thank you, friend," said Arion.

"A poor favor to return for such heavenly music," said the dolphin as he swam away with Arion on his back.

The other dolphins danced along on the water, as Arion played. They swam very swiftly and brought Arion to Corinth a day before the ship was due. He went immediately to his friend, Periander, king of Corinth, and told him his story. Then he took the king down to the waterfront to introduce him to the dolphin that had saved his life. The dolphin, who had become very fond of Arion, longed to stay with him in Corinth. So the king had the river dammed up to make a giant pool on the palace grounds, and there the dolphin stayed when he wished to visit Arion.

When the thieves' ship arrived in port, captain and crew were seized by the king's guard and taken to the castle. Arion stayed hidden.

"Why have you taken us captive, oh king?" said the captain. "We are peaceable law-abiding sailors."

"My friend Arion took passage on your ship!" roared the king. "Where is he? What have you done with him?"

"Poor lad," said the captain. "He was quite mad. He was on deck singing to himself one day, and then suddenly jumped overboard. We put out a small boat, circled the spot for hours. We couldn't find a trace. Sharks probably. Sea's full of them there."

"And what do you do to a man-eating shark when you catch him?" asked the king.

"Kill him, of course," said the captain. "We can't let them swim free and eat other sailors."

"A noble sentiment," said Arion, stepping out of his hiding place. "That's exactly what we do to two-legged sharks in Corinth."

So the captain and his crew were taken out and hanged. The ship was searched and Arion found all that had been taken from him. He insisted on dividing the gifts with the king. When Periander protested, Arion laughed and said: "Treasures are trouble. You're a king and can handle them. But I'm a minstrel and must travel light."

And all his life Arion sang songs of praise. His music grew in power and beauty until people said he was a second Orpheus. When he died Apollo set him in the sky — and his lyre, and the dolphin too. They shine in the night sky still, the stars of constellations we still call the Lyre and the Dolphin.

The Gift of Fire

Prometheus was a bold young giant who insisted on finding things out for himself. He feared no one, not even Zeus, who ruled the gods on Mount Olympus and the men on earth, and kept everyone frightened with his mighty thunderbolt. Prometheus knew how much the powerful god hated questions about his rule, but the young giant asked them anyway when there was something he wanted to know.

One morning he walked up to Zeus and said, "Oh, thunderer, I do not understand. You have put men on earth, but you keep them in fear and darkness."

"Perhaps you had better leave all matters con-

7

cerning man to me," said Zeus in a warning tone. "Their fear, as you call it, is simply respect for the gods. The 'darkness' is the peaceful shadow of my law. Man is happy now. And he will remain happy — unless someone tells him he is *un*happy. Let us not speak of this again."

But Prometheus persisted. "Look at man!" he said. "Look below. There he crouches in cold dark caves. He is at the mercy of the beasts and the weather. He even eats his meat raw. Tell me why you refuse to give man the gift of fire."

Zeus answered, "Don't you know, Prometheus, that every gift has a price? And the cost of the gift is usually more than it is worth. Man does not have fire, true. He has not learned the crafts which go with fire. But he is lucky all the same. He does not suffer disease, or warfare, or old age, or that inward sickness called worry. He is quite happy without fire. And so, I say, he shall remain."

"Man is happy the way animals are happy," retorted Prometheus. "What was the sense of creating this race called man if he must live like the beasts, without fire? He doesn't even have any fur to keep him warm."

"He is different from the beasts in other ways," said Zeus. "Man needs someone to worship. And we gods need someone to worship us. That is why man was made."

"But wouldn't fire and the things that fire can do for him make him more interesting?"

"More interesting, perhaps, but much more dangerous. Like the gods, man is full of pride. It would take very little to make this pride swell to giant size. If I improve man's lot, he will forget the very thing which makes him so pleasing to us: his need to worship and obey. He will become poisoned with pride and begin to fancy that he himself is a god. Before we know it he will be storming Mount Olympus. You have said enough, Prometheus. I have been patient with you. Do not try me too far. Go now, and trouble me no more with your questions."

But Prometheus was not satisfied. All that night he lay awake making plans. When dawn came he left his bed and, standing tiptoe on Olympus, stretched his arm to the eastern horizon, where the first faint flames of the sun were flickering. In his hand he held a reed filled with dry fiber. He thrust it into the sunrise until a spark smouldered. Then he put the reed in his tunic and came down from the mountain.

At first, men were frightened by his gift. It was so hot, so quick. It bit sharply when you touched it, and set the shadows dancing. The men thanked Prometheus, but they asked him to take away his gift.

But instead Prometheus took the haunch of a

newly killed deer and held it over the fire. When the meat began to sear and sputter, filling the cave with the rich smell of roasting venison, the people went mad with hunger. They flung themselves on the meat, and ate greedily, burning their tongues.

"That which cooked the meat is called fire," Prometheus told them. "It is an ill-natured spirit, a little brother of the sun, but if you handle it carefully it can change your whole life. You must feed it with twigs — but only until it is big enough to roast your meat or heat your cave. Then you must stop, or it will eat everything in sight, and you too. If it escapes, use this magic — water. If you touch it with water it will shrink to the right size again."

Prometheus left the fire burning in the first cave, and the children stared at it, wide-eyed. Then he went to every cave in the land, bringing his gift of fire.

For some time afterward, Zeus was kept busy with the affairs of the gods. Then, one day, he looked down from Mt. Olympus, and was amazed. Everything had changed. Zeus saw woodsmen's huts, farmhouses, villages, walled towns, even a castle or two. He saw men cooking their food and carrying torches to light their way at night. He saw forges blazing, men beating out ploughs, keels, swords, spears. They were making ships and raising white winds of sails, daring to use the fury of the winds for their journeys. They were even wearing helmets, and riding out to do battle — like the gods themselves.

Zeus was very angry. He seized his largest thunderbolt. "So men want fire," he said to himself. "I'll give them fire — more than they can use. I'll burn their miserable little ball of earth to a cinder."

But then another thought came to him and he lowered his arm. "No," he said to himself. "I'll attend to these mortals later. My first business is with Prometheus. And when I finish with him no one else — man, god, or giant — will dare to disobey me."

Zeus then called his guards and had them seize Prometheus. He ordered them to drag him off to the far north. There they bound Prometheus to a mountain peak with great chains specially forged by the god of fire. These chains were so strong that even a giant could not break them, no matter how hard he struggled. When the friend of man was bound to the mountain, Zeus sent two vultures to hover about him forever, tearing at his vitals, and eating his liver.

Men knew that a terrible thing was happening on the mountain, but they did not know what it was. They could hear the wind shriek like a giant in torment, and sometimes like fierce birds.

For centuries Prometheus lay there helpless — until another hero was born, brave enough to defy the gods. He climbed the mountain peak, struck the chains from Prometheus, and killed the vultures. His name was Hercules.

And so, at last, man was able to repay Prometheus for his great gift — the gift of fire.

The Mysterious Box

Zeus brooded. He could not forget how Prometheus had dared to break his law and teach man the use of fire. After the lord of the sky had punished Prometheus with an endless torment for giving man fire, he began to plan how to punish man for accepting the gift. He thought and brooded, and finally he hit upon a plan.

"A good scheme," he told himself. "It will give me vengeance and entertainment as well. Of course there is always a chance that the girl will resist temptation and save mankind. But I'll take that risk."

He ordered the fire god to mold a girl out of clay. Then Zeus breathed life into the clay girl.

13

The clay turned to flesh, and a maiden lay sleeping before him. Then he called the gods together, and asked them each to give her a special gift, and told them what he wanted those gifts to be.

Apollo taught her to sing and play the lyre. Athena taught her to spin. Ceres taught her how to plant seeds and make things grow. Venus gave her the gift of beauty and taught her to dance. Neptune gave her the power to change herself into a mermaid so that she could swim in the stormiest seas without drowning. Mercury gave her a beautiful golden box. But he told her she must never, never open it. And, finally, Hera gave her the tricky gift of curiosity.

Mercury took her by the hand and led her down the slope of Mount Olympus. He led her to the brother of Prometheus and said, "Father Zeus regrets the disgrace which has fallen upon your family. And to show you that he doesn't blame you for your brother's crime, he offers you this girl to be your wife. She is the fairest maid in all the world. Her name is Pandora, the all-gifted."

So the brother of Prometheus married Pandora. She spun and baked and tended her garden, and played the lyre and danced for her husband. For a while they were the happiest young couple on earth.

But from the first Pandora could not help

thinking about the golden box. She was very proud of it. She kept it on the table and polished it every day. But the box sparkled in the sunlight and seemed to be winking at her. She could not help wondering what was inside.

She began to talk to herself in this way: "Mercury must have been teasing. He's always making jokes; everyone knows that. Yes, he was teasing me, telling me never to open his gift. If it is so beautiful outside, what a treasure there must be inside! Diamonds and sapphires and rubies more lovely than anyone has ever seen. After all, it is a gift from the hand of a god. If the box is so rich, the gift inside must be even more splendid. Perhaps Mercury really expects me to open the box and tell him how delighted I am with his gift. Perhaps he's waiting for me to thank him. He probably thinks I'm ungrateful."

But even as she was telling herself all this, she knew in her heart that it was not so. The box must *not* be opened. She *must* keep her promise.

Finally, she knew she had to do something to stop herself from thinking about the box. She took it from the table, and hid it in a dusty little storeroom. But it seemed to be burning there in the shadows. It scorched her thoughts wherever she went. She kept passing that room and stepping into it and making excuses to dawdle there.

Once she took the box from its hiding place and stroked it — then quickly shoved it out of sight and rushed from the room.

After some days of this torment, she locked the golden box in a heavy oak chest. She put great bolts on the chest, and dug a hole in her garden. Then she put the chest in the hole and covered it over — and rolled a boulder on top of it. When her husband came home that night, her hair was wild and her hands were bloody, and her tunic was torn and stained. But all she would tell him was that she had been working in the garden.

That night the moonlight blazed in the room. Pandora could not sleep. She sat up in bed and looked around. All the room was swimming in moonlight. Everything was different. There were deep shadows and bright patches of silver, all mixed, all moving. She arose quietly and tiptoed from the room.

She went out into the garden. The trees were swaying. The whole world was adance in the magic white fire of moonlight. She felt full of wild strength. She walked over to the rock and pushed. The rock rolled away as lightly as a pebble. Then she took a shovel and dug down to the chest. She unfastened the bolts and drew out the golden box. It was cold, cold! The coldness burned her hand to the bone. She trembled, not

16

with cold, but with fear. She felt that the box held the very secret of life. She must look inside or die.

Pandora took a little golden key from her tunic, fitted it into the keyhole, and gently opened the lid. There was a swarming, a wild throbbing, a nameless rustling, and a horrid sickening smell. Out of the box, as she held it up in the moonlight, swarmed small, scaly, lizardlike creatures with bat wings and burning red eyes.

They flew out of the box, circled her head once, clapping their wings and screaming thin little jeering screams. Then they flew off into the night, hissing and cackling.

Half fainting, Pandora sank to her knees. With her last bit of strength she clutched the box and shut down the lid, catching the last little monster just as it was wriggling free. It shrieked and spat and clawed her hand, but she thrust it back into the box and locked it in. Then she dropped the box and fainted away.

What were those loathsome creatures that flew out of the golden box? They were all the ills that trouble mankind; the spites and jealousies, disease of every kind, old age, famine, drought, poverty, war, and all the evils that bring grief and misery. After they flew out of the box, they scattered. They flew into every home, and swung from the rafters, waiting. And even today, when their time comes, they swoop down and sting, bringing pain and sorrow and death to men and women everywhere.

But bad as they were, things could have been worse. For the creature that Pandora managed to shut in the box was the worst of all. It was Foreboding, the knowledge of misfortune to come. If it had flown free, people would know ahead of time every terrible thing that was to happen to them throughout their lives. Hope would have died. And that would have been the death of man as well. For people can bear endless trouble, but they cannot live without hope.

Narcissus and Echo

Echo was the best beloved of all the nymphs of river and woods. She was not only very beautiful and very kind, but she had a hauntingly beautiful voice. All the children of the villages used to come into the woods to beg her to sing to them and tell them stories.

One day as Echo sat among a circle of wide-eyed boys and girls, telling them stories of heroes and gods and monsters, a handsome young woodsman, all dressed in green, came into the grove. He was carrying a bulging sack over his shoulder.

Now Echo didn't know this, but the young

woodsman was Zeus, king of the gods, in disguise. Occasionally Zeus liked to change into human form and wander the earth. He waited, enchanted by Echo's voice, until she finished her tale, and then said, "Well told, beautiful maiden! I have a present for you and for each boy and girl."

He opened the sack. It was full of golden apples — solid gold and heavy and shining. He gave one to Echo and one each to the children, who began to play ball with them, tossing them from one to another. In the midst of their play the woodsman disappeared.

Echo knew now that the woodsman was Zeus, for she recognized the golden apples which grew on a magic tree belonging to Zeus' wife, Hera. Echo also knew that Hera, who was not as kind as Zeus, would be very angry when she learned that her husband was giving away her precious golden apples. Echo couldn't wait to tell the news to her friend Venus, goddess of love and beauty.

The next day she told Venus how Zeus had come to the grove disguised as a woodsman and given away Hera's golden apples. "See, he gave me one too," she said, tossing it up in the air so that it flashed in the sunlight.

"You'd better hide that, my child," said Venus.

"Why? It's so beautiful. I don't want to hide it. I want to look at it."

"Take my advice," said Venus. "Hide it. Hera is very jealous. She knows what Zeus has done and she is furious."

Poor Echo was soon to learn how dangerous it was to make Hera angry. For the queen of the gods sent her spies everywhere. And very soon she learned that Zeus had given one of her precious golden apples to a wood nymph named Echo.

"Echo, eh?" snarled Hera. "That little tree toad who thinks she's a nightingale? Well, I'll make her sorry she ever laid eyes on a golden apple. I'll punish her in a way that will be remembered forever."

Hera strode down from Olympus, muttering to herself, scowling, black hair flying. This happened on a day that Venus was visiting Echo. They were sitting comfortably in the woods on a fallen log, chatting.

"All the world asks me for favors," Venus said. "But not you, Echo. Tell me, isn't there someone you want to love you? Just name him, and I will send my son, Cupid, to shoot him with an arrow, and make him fall madly in love with you."

But Echo laughed, and said, "Alas, sweet Venus, I have seen no boy who pleases me. None seems beautiful enough to match my secret dream. When the time comes I shall ask your help — if it ever comes."

"Well, you are lovely enough to have the best," said Venus. "And remember, I am always at your service."

Now Echo did not know this, but at that very moment the most beautiful boy in the whole world was lost in that very wood. His name was Narcissus. He was so handsome that he had never been able to speak to any woman except his mother, for any girl who saw him immediately fainted. Because of this he had a very high opinion of himself. As he went through the woods, he thought: "Oh, how I wish I could find someone as beautiful as I am. I will not love anyone less perfect in face or form than myself. Why should I? This makes me lonely, it's true. But it's better than lowering myself."

As he walked along talking to himself, Narcissus was getting more and more lost in the woods. In another part of that wood, Echo had just said farewell to Venus, and was going back to the hollow tree in which she lived. As she came to a clearing in the forest, she saw something that made her stop in astonishment and hide behind a tree. What she saw was a tall, purple-clad figure moving through the trees. She recognized Hera, and hurried forward to curtsy low before the queen of the gods. "Greetings, great queen," Echo said. "Welcome to the wood."

"Wretched creature!" Hera cried. "I know how you tricked my husband! Well, I have a gift for you too. Because you used your voice to bewitch my husband, you shall never be able to say anything again — except the last words that have been said to you. Now, try babbling."

"Try babbling," said Echo.

"No more shall you chat with your betters. No more shall you gossip, tell stories or sing songs. You shall endure this punishment forever."

"Forever," said Echo, sobbing.

Then Hera went away to search for Zeus. Echo, weeping, rushed toward her home in the hollow tree. As she was running she saw a dazzling brightness that she thought was the face of a god, and she stopped to look. But it was no god. It was a boy about her own age, with yellow hair and eyes the color of sapphires. When she saw him, all the pain of her punishment dissolved and she was full of great laughing joy. Here was the boy she had been looking for all her life. He was a boy as beautiful as her secret dream — a boy she could love.

Echo danced toward him. He stopped and said, "Pardon me, but can you show me the path out of the wood?"

"Out of the wood?" said Echo.

"Yes," he said. "I'm lost. I've been wandering here for hours and I can't seem to find my way out of the wood."

"Out of the wood."

"Yes, I've told you twice. I'm lost. Can you help me find the way?"

"The way?"

"Are you deaf, perhaps? Why must I repeat everything?"

"Repeat everything?"

"No, I will not. It's a bore. I won't do it."

"Do it."

"Look, I can't stand here arguing with you. If you don't want to show me the way, I'll just try to find someone who can."

"Who can."

Narcissus glared at her and turned away. But Echo went to him, and put her arms around him, and tried to kiss his face.

"Oh, no!" said Narcissus, pushing her away. "Stop it! You can't kiss me."

"Kiss me."

"No!"

"No!"

Again Echo tried to kiss Narcissus, but he pushed her aside. She fell on her knees on the path, and lifting her lovely tearstained face, tried to speak to him. But she could not. She reached up and grasped his hand.

"Let go!" he said. "You cannot hold me here. I will not love you."

"Love you."

Narcissus tore himself from her grip and strode away. "Farewell."

"Farewell."

Echo looked after Narcissus until he disappeared. And when he was gone she felt such sadness, such terrible tearing grief, that it seemed as if she was being torn apart. And since she could not speak out, she offered up this prayer silently:

"Oh, Venus, fair goddess, you promised me a favor. Hear me now, though I am voiceless. My love has disappeared and I want to disappear too, for I cannot bear this pain."

Venus, in the garden on Mount Olympus, heard Echo's prayer, for prayers do not have to be spoken to be heard. She looked down upon the grieving nymph, and pitied her, and made her disappear. Echo's body melted into thin cool air, so that the pain was gone. All was gone except her voice, for Venus could not bear to lose that lovely sound. The goddess said:

"I grant you your wish — and one thing more. You have not asked vengeance upon the love that has made you suffer. You are too sweet and kind. But *I* shall take vengeance. I decree that whoever caused you this pain will know the same terrible longing. He will fall in love with someone who cannot return his love. And he will seek forever for what he can never have."

Now Narcissus knew nothing of this. He was not aware of Echo's grief, or the vow of Venus. He still wandered the forest path, thinking, "These girls who love me on sight — it's too bad I cannot find one as beautiful as I am. Until I do, I shall not love."

Finally he sank down on the bank of a river to rest. Not a river really, but a finger of the river — a clear little stream moving slowly through the rocks. The sun shone on the water so that it became a mirror, holding the trees and the sky upside down. And Narcissus, looking into the stream, saw a face.

He blinked at the water again. It was still there — the most beautiful face he had ever seen. As beautiful, he knew, as his own, even though the shimmer of light behind it made it slightly blurred. He gazed and gazed at the face. He could not have enough of it. He knew that he could look upon this face forever. He put out his hand to touch it. The water trembled, and the face disappeared.

"A water nymph," he thought. "A lovely daughter of the river god. The loveliest of his daughters, no doubt. She is shy. Like me, she can't bear to be touched. Ah, here she is again."

The face looked up at him out of the stream. Again, very timidly, he reached out his hand. Again the water trembled and the face disappeared.

"I will stay here until she loves me," he thought. "She may hide now, but soon she will love me and come out." And he said aloud, "Come out, lovely one."

And the voice of Echo, who had followed him to the stream, said, "Lovely one."

"Hear that, hear that!" cried Narcissus, overjoyed. "She cares for me too. You do, don't you? You love me."

"Love me."

"I do. I do," cried Narcissus. "Finally, I have found someone I love. Come out, come out. Oh, will you never come out?"

"Never come out?" said Echo.

"Don't say that, please don't say that. Because I will stay here till you do. This, I vow."

"I vow."

"Your voice is as beautiful as your face. And I will stay here adoring you forever."

"Forever."

And Narcissus stayed there, leaning over the stream, watching the face in the water. Sometimes he pleaded with it to come out, coaxing, begging, always looking. But day after day he stayed there; night after night, never moving, never eating, never looking away from that face.

Narcissus stayed there so long that his legs grew into the bank of the river and became roots. His hair grew long, tangled, and leafy, and his pale face became delicate yellow and white. He became the flower Narcissus that lives on the river bank, and leans over watching its reflection in the water.

You can find him there to this day. And in the woods, when all is still, in certain valleys and high places, you can sometimes come upon Echo. And if you call her in a certain way, she will answer your call.

Wild Horses of the Sun

The two young boys had been wrestling, boxing, and shooting arrows at a tree stump all day long. The black-haired boy was a son of Zeus. The yellow-haired one, named Phaeton, was a son of Apollo. But, as it happened, neither of them had ever met his father.

When the boys grew tired of the games, they sat down on the edge of a cliff, dangling their legs over the blue sea, and began boasting and lying to each other. This was a very long time ago and most things have changed — but not boys.

"My father is Zeus," said the black-haired boy. "He's the chief god, lord of the mountain, king of the sky."

"My father is lord of the sun," said Phaeton.

"My father is called the thunderer," replied the other. "When he is angry, the sky grows black and the sun hides. His spear is a lightning bolt. That's what he kills people with. He can hurl it a thousand miles and never miss."

"Without my father there would be no day," said Phaeton. "It would always be night. Each morning he drives the golden chariot of the sun across the sky, bringing the daytime. Then he dives into the ocean, boards a golden ferryboat, and sails back to his eastern palace. Then it is nighttime."

"When I visit my father," said the black-haired boy, "he gives me presents. Do you know what he gave me last time? A thunderbolt — a little one, but just like his. And he taught me how to throw it. I killed three vultures, scared a fishing boat, and started a forest fire. Next time I go to see him, I'll throw it at more things. Do you visit your father?"

Phaeton never had, but he wasn't going to admit it. "Certainly," he said. "All the time. And he teaches me things too."

"What kinds of things? Has he taught you to drive the sun chariot?"

"Oh, yes. He taught me how to handle the horses of the sun, how to make them go, and how to make them stop. They're huge wild horses and they breathe fire."

"I bet you made all that up," said the black-haired boy. "I don't believe there is a sun chariot. There's the sun, look at it. It's not a chariot."

"What you see is just one of the wheels," said Phaeton. "There's another wheel on the other side, and the body of the chariot is slung between them. That is where my father stands and drives his horses."

"All right, so it's a chariot," said the black-haired boy. "But I still don't believe your father would let you drive it. In fact, I don't think Apollo would know you if he saw you. Maybe he isn't even your father. People like to say they're descended from the gods — but how many of us are there, really?"

"I'll prove it to you," cried Phaeton, scrambling to his feet. "I'll go to the palace of the sun right now and hold my father to his promise."

"What promise?"

"He said that the next time I visited him he would let me drive the sun chariot all by myself, because I was getting so good at it. I'll show you. I'll drive the sun right across the sky."

"That's easy for you to say," said the other. "But how will I know if you're driving the sun? I won't be able to see you from down here."

"You'll know me," said Phaeton. "I'll come down close and drive in circles over the village. Just watch the sky tomorrow."

Phaeton went off then. He traveled day and night, not stopping for food or rest, guiding himself by the stars, heading always east. He walked on and on and on until, finally, he had lost his way completely.

While Phaeton was making his journey, Apollo was sitting in his great throne room. It was the quiet hour before dawn, when night had dropped its last coolness upon the earth. At this hour, Apollo always sat on his throne. He wore a purple cloak embroidered with golden stars, and a crown made of silver and pearls. Suddenly a bird flew in the window and perched on his shoulder. This bird had sky-blue feathers, a golden beak, golden claws, and golden eyes. It was one of Apollo's sun hawks, whose job it was to fly here and there gathering information. Sometimes they were called spy birds.

Now the bird spoke to Apollo. "I have seen your son," she said.

"Which son?"

"Phaeton. He was coming to see you. But he lost his way and lies exhausted at the edge of a wood. The wolves will surely kill him."

"Then we'd better get to him before the wolves do," said Apollo. "Round up some of your flock and bear Phaeton here in a manner that befits the son of a god."

The sun hawk then seized the softly glowing rug at the foot of the throne and flew away with it. She called to three other hawks to each hold a corner of the rug. They flew over a river and a mountain and a wood and finally came to the field where Phaeton lay. They flew down among the howling wolves, among the burning eyes set in a circle about the sleeping boy. They rolled Phaeton onto the rug, and then each took a corner of the rug in her beak again, and flew away.

Phaeton felt himself being lifted into the air. The cold wind woke him up, and he sat up straight. The people below saw a boy, with folded arms, sitting on a carpet that was rushing through the cold bright moonlight far above their heads. And that is why we hear tales of flying carpets even to this day.

Phaeton remembered lying down on the grass to sleep, and now, he knew, he was dreaming. And when he saw the great cloud castle on top of the mountain, all made of snow and rosy in the early light, he was surer than ever that he was dreaming. He saw sentries in flashing golden armor, carrying golden spears. In the courtyard he saw enormous woolly dogs with fleece like cloud-drift guarding the gate.

Over the wall flew the carpet, over the court-yard, through the huge doors. And it wasn't until the sun hawks gently let down the carpet in front of the throne that Phaeton began to think that this dream might be very real. He raised his eyes shyly and saw a tall figure sitting on the throne—taller than anyone Phaeton had ever seen, with golden hair and stormy blue eyes and a strong laughing face. Phaeton fell on his knees.

"Father!" he cried. "I am Phaeton, your son!"

"Rise, Phaeton. Let me look at you."

The boy stood up. His legs were trembling.

"Well, boy, what brings you here?" said Apollo. "Don't you know that you should wait for an invitation before visiting a god — even your father?"

"I had no choice, Father. I was jeered at by a son of Zeus. He was bragging about his father, so I did a little bragging and lying too. I would have thrown him over the cliff, and myself after him, if I hadn't decided to make my lies come true."

"Well, you're my son, all right," said Apollo. "Proud, rash, taking every dare, refusing no adventure. Speak up, then. What is it you wish? I will do anything in my power to help you."

"Anything, Father?"

"Anything in my power. I swear by the River Styx, an oath sacred to the gods."

"I wish to drive the sun across the sky. All by myself. From dawn till night."

Apollo's roar of anger shattered every crystal goblet in the great castle.

"Impossible!" he cried. "No one can drive those horses but me. They are tall as mountains and wild as tigers. They are stronger than the tides, stronger than the winds. It is all that I can do to hold them in check. How could your puny grip control them? They will race away with the chariot, scorching the poor earth to a cinder."

"You promised, Father. You swore by the River Styx!"

"You must not hold me to my oath. If you do, it will be a death sentence for earth...a poor charred cinder floating in space...just what the Fates have said would happen. But I did not know it would be so soon, so soon."

"It is almost dawn, Father. Can we harness the horses?"

"Please, Phaeton. Ask me anything else and I will grant it. But do not ask me this."

"I have asked, Sire, and you have given your oath. The horses grow restless."

"I will do as you ask," said Apollo. "Come."

He led Phaeton to the stable of the sun where

the giant horses were being harnessed to the golden chariot. Huge they were. Red and gold and fire-maned, with golden hooves and hot yellow eyes. When they neighed, the sound rolled across the sky. Their breath was flame.

The sun chariot was an open shell of gold. Each wheel was the flat round disc of the sun, as it is seen in the sky. Phaeton looked very small as he stood in the chariot. The reins were thick as bridge cables, much too large for him to hold, so Apollo tied them around his son's waist. Then Apollo stood at the head of the team, gentling the horses, speaking softly to them.

"Good horses, go easy today. Go at a slow trot, my swift ones, and do not leave the path. You have a new driver today."

The great horses dropped their heads to Apollo's shoulder, and whinnied softly, for they loved him. Phaeton saw the flame of their breath play about his father's head. He saw Apollo's face shining out of the flame. But Apollo was not harmed, for he was a god and could not be hurt by physical things.

Then Apollo came to Phaeton and said, "Listen to me, my son. You are about to start a terrible journey, and by the obedience you owe me as a son, by the faith you owe a god, by my oath that cannot be broken, and your pride that will not bend, I ask you this. Keep to the middle way. If you go too high the earth will freeze. If you go too low it will burn. Keep to the middle way. Give the horses their heads; they know the path — the blue middle course of day. Don't drive them too high or too low, and above all do not stop. If you do, you will fire the air about you, charring the earth and blistering the sky. Will you heed me?"

"I will, I will!" cried Phaeton. "Stand away, Sire. The dawn grows old and day must begin! Go, horses, go!"

And Apollo stood watching as the horses of the sun, pulling behind them the golden chariot, climbed the eastern slope of the sky.

At first things went well for Phaeton. The great steeds trotted easily across the high blue meadow of the sky. Phaeton thought to himself, "I can't understand why my father made such a fuss. This is easy. There is nothing to it."

When he looked over the edge of the chariot, he could see tiny houses far below, specks of trees, and a dark blue puddle that was the sea. The coach was trundling across the sky. The great sun wheels were turning, casting light, warming and brightening the earth, chasing away the shadows of night.

"Just imagine," Phaeton thought, "people are

looking up at the sky, praising the sun, hoping the weather stays fair. How many are watching me?" Then he thought, "But I'm too small for them to see, too far away. And the light of the sun is too bright. For all they know, I could be Apollo making his usual run. How will they know it's me, *me, me*, if I can't go closer? Especially Zeus' son — how will *he* know? I'll go home tomorrow, and tell him what I did, and he'll laugh at me and say I'm lying, just as he did before. No! I must show him that I am driving the chariot of the sun. Apollo said not to drive too close to earth, but how will he know? I won't stay long. I'll just dip down toward our village and circle it a few times until everyone recognizes me."

When they were over the village where Phaeton lived, he jerked on the reins, pulling the horses' heads down. They whinnied angrily, and tossed their heads, but he jerked the reins again.

"Down!" he cried. "Down! Down!"

The horses plunged down through the bright air, their golden hooves twinkling, their golden manes flying. They pulled the great glittering chariot over the village in a long flaming swoop. Phaeton was horrified to see the houses burst into fire. The trees burned like torches. And people rushed about screaming, their loose clothing on fire.

Phaeton could not see because of the smoke. Had he burned his own home — and his mother and sisters? He threw himself backward in the chariot, pulling at the reins with all his might, shouting "Up! Up!"

The horses, made furious by the smoke, reared on their hind legs. They leaped upward, galloping through the smoke, pulling the chariot up, up.

Swiftly the earth fell away beneath them until the village was just a smudge of smoke. Again Phaeton saw the pencil-stroke of mountain, the inkblot of sea. "Whoa!" he cried. "Turn now! Forward on your path!"

But he could no longer handle the horses. They were galloping, not trotting. They had taken the bit in their teeth. They did not turn toward the path of the day — across the meadow of the sky — but galloped up and up. And the people on earth saw the sun shooting away until it was no larger than a star.

Then darkness came, and cold. The earth froze hard. Rivers froze, and the oceans too. Boats were caught fast in the ice, and it snowed in the jungle. Marble buildings cracked. It was impossible for anyone to speak, for their breath froze on their lips. In villages and cities, in fields and in woods, people died of the cold. Their bodies were piled up like firewood.

Still Phaeton could not hold the horses, and still they galloped upward dragging light and warmth away from the earth. Finally, they had gone so high that the air was too thin for them to breathe. Phaeton saw the flame of their breath, which had been red and yellow, burn blue in the thin air. He himself was gasping for breath, and he felt the marrow of his bones freezing.

The horses, maddened by the feeble hand on the reins, swung around and dived toward earth again. As they galloped downward, all the ice melted, causing great floods. Whole villages were swept away by a solid wall of water. Trees were uprooted and forests were torn away. Still the horses swooped lower and lower. Now the water began to boil — great billowing clouds of steam arose.

Phaeton could not see; the steam was too thick. He untied the reins from his waist, for they would have cut him in two. He had no control over the horses at all. They galloped upward again, out of the steam, taking at last the middle way in the sky. But they raced wildly, using all their tremendous strength. They circled the earth in a matter of minutes, smashing across the sky from horizon to horizon. They made the day flash on and off, like someone playing with a lantern. And the people who were left alive were bewildered by day and night following each other so swiftly.

Up high on Olympus, the gods in their cool garden heard the clamor of grief from below. Zeus looked down on earth and saw the runaway horses of the sun and the hurtling chariot. He saw the dead and the dying, the burning forests, the floods, the strange frost. Then he looked again at the chariot and saw that it was not Apollo who was driving, but someone he did not know. He stood up, drew back his arm, and hurled a thunderbolt.

It stabbed through the air, striking Phaeton and killing him instantly. The boy was knocked out of the chariot, and his body, flaming, fell like a star. The horses of the sun, knowing themselves driverless now, galloped homeward toward their stables at the eastern edge of the sky.

Since that day, no one has been allowed to drive the chariot of the sun except the sun god himself. But there are still traces on earth of Phaeton's reckless ride. The ends of the earth are still covered with ice caps. Mountains still rumble, trying to spit out the fire that was started in their bellies by the diving sun. And where the horses of the sun swung too close to earth, are the great scorched places called deserts.

The Solid Gold Princess

Once there was a king named Midas, and what
he loved best in all the world was gold. He had
plenty of his own, but he could not bear the
thought of anyone else having any. One morning
he happened to wake at dawn and, watching
Apollo driving his sun chariot along the slope of
the sky, he said to himself, "Of all the gods I like
you least, Apollo. How dare you be so wasteful,
scattering golden light on rich and poor alike —
on king and peasant, on merchant, shepherd,
sailor? Don't you understand that only kings
should have gold; only the rich know what to do
with it?"

Midas did not mean his words to be heard, but
the gods have sharp ears. Apollo did hear, and

was very angry. That night he came to Midas in a dream and said, "Other gods would punish you, Midas, but I am famous for my good nature. Instead of harming you, I will do you a kindness and grant your dearest wish. What is it to be?"

Midas cried, "Let everything I touch turn to gold!"

He shouted this out in a strangling greedy voice. The guards at his doorway nodded to each other and said, "The king calls out. He must be dreaming of gold again."

Midas awoke in a bad mood. "Oh, if it were only true," he said to himself, "and everything I touch turned to gold. What's the use of such dreams? They only tease and torment a man."

That morning as he was walking in the garden, his hand brushed a rose. Amazed, he watched it turn to gold. Petals and stalk, it turned to gold and stood there, rigid, heavy, gleaming. A bee buzzed out of its stiff folds and, furious, lit on the king's hand to sting him. The king looked at the heavy golden bee on the back of his hand and moved it to his finger.

"I shall wear it as a ring," he said.

Then he hurried about the garden, touching all the roses, watching them stiffen and gleam. They lost their odor. The disappointed bees rose in swarms and buzzed angrily away. Butterflies departed. The flowers tinkled like lttle bells when the breeze moved among them, and the king was well pleased.

His little daughter, the princess, who had been playing in the garden, ran to him and said, "Father, Father, what has happened to the roses?"

"Are they not pretty, my dear?"

"No! They're ugly! They're horrid and sharp and I can't smell them any more! What happened?"

"A magical thing."

"Who did the magic?"

"I did."

"Unmagic it then! I hate these roses," she said, and began to cry.

"Don't cry," he said, stroking her head. "Stop crying and I will give you a golden doll with a gold-leaf dress and tiny golden shoes."

The princess stopped crying, and Midas felt her hair grow spiky under his fingers. Her eyes stiffened and froze into place. The little blue vein in her neck stopped pulsing. She was a statue, a figure of pale gold standing in the garden path. Her tears were tiny golden beads on her golden cheeks.

Midas looked at his daughter and said, "Oh, my dear, I'm sorry. But I have no time to be sad this morning. I shall be busy turning things into gold. When I have a moment I'll think about your problem, I promise."

He hurried out of the garden. On his way back to the castle he amused himself by kicking up gravel and watching it tinkle down as tiny nuggets. The door he opened became golden. The chair he sat upon became solid gold like his throne. The plates turned into gold, and the cups became gold cups before the amazed eyes of his servants, whom Midas was careful not to touch. He wanted them to keep on serving him.

Greedily he bit into a piece of bread and honey. But his teeth clanked on metal — his mouth was full of metal. He felt himself choking. He plucked from his mouth a piece of gold which had been bread. Very lightly then he touched the other food to see what would happen. Meat...apples...walnuts...all turned to gold, even when he touched them with only the tip of his finger. When he did not touch the food with his fingers, but lifted it on his fork, it became gold as soon as it touched his lips. He was savagely hungry now.

But worse than hunger was the thought of drinking. He realized that wine, or water, or milk would turn to gold in his mouth, and choke him if he swallowed.

"What good is all my gold," he cried, "if I cannot eat and cannot drink?"

Midas shrieked with rage, pounded on the table, and flung the plates about. Then he raced out of the castle and along the golden gravel path to the garden, where the stiff flowers chimed hatefully. The statue of his daughter looked at him with scooped and empty eyes. In the blaze of the sun, Midas raised his arms heavenward and cried, "You, Apollo, false god, traitor! You pretended to forgive me, but you punished me with a gift!"

Then it seemed to Midas that the sun grew brighter, and that the sun god stood before him on the path, tall, stern, clad in burning gold. A voice said, "On your knees, wretch!"

Midas fell to his knees.

"Have you learned anything?"

"I have...I have...I will never desire gold again. I will never accuse the gods. Please take back the fatal gift."

Apollo reached out his hand and touched the roses. The tinkling stopped. The flowers softened and swayed and blushed. Fragrance grew on the air again. And the bees returned, and the butterflies. Apollo touched the statue's cheek. It lost its stiffness, its metallic gleam. The princess ran to the roses, knelt among them, and cried, "Oh, thank you, Father. You've changed them back again." Then she ran off, shouting and laughing.

Apollo said, "I take back my gift, Midas. Your touch is cleansed of its golden curse. But you may not escape without punishment. Because you have been the most foolish of men, you shall wear a pair of donkey's ears."

Midas touched his ears. They were long and furry. He said, "I thank you for your forgiveness, Apollo...even though it comes with a punishment."

Apollo said, "Eat and drink. Enjoy the roses. Watch your child grow. And remember, life is the greatest wealth. In your stupidity you have been wasteful of life, and that is the sign you wear on your head. Farewell."

Midas put a tall pointed hat on his head so that no one would see his ears. Then he went to eat and drink his fill.

For years Midas wore the cap so that no one would know of his disgrace. But the servant who cut his hair had to know, so Midas made him swear not to tell. He warned the servant that it would cost him his head if he spoke of the king's ears. But the servant was a gossip. He could not bear to keep a secret, especially such a secret about the king. He was afraid to tell it, but he also felt that he would burst if he did not.

So one night he went down to the bank of the river, dug a little hole, put his mouth to the hole, and whispered, "Midas has donkey's ears...Midas has donkey's ears." Quickly he filled up the hole again, and ran back to the castle feeling better.

But the reeds on the riverbank had heard him, and they always whisper to each other when the wind blows. They were heard whispering, "Midas has donkey's ears...donkey's ears..." Soon the whole country was whispering, "Have you heard about Midas? Have you heard about his ears?"

When the king heard, he knew who had told the secret. He ordered the man's head cut off. But then he thought, "Apollo forgave me. Perhaps I had better forgive this blabbermouth." And he let the man keep his head.

Then Apollo appeared to the king again and said, "Midas, you have learned the final lesson, mercy. As you have done, so shall you be done by."

And as Apollo spoke Midas felt his long hairy ears shrinking back to the right size.

When he was an old man, Midas would tell his smallest granddaughter the story of how her mother was turned into a golden statue. "See, I'm changing you too," he would say. "Look, your hair is all gold."

And she pretended to be frightened.

The Dragon's Teeth

Long ago, when the world was very new, people believed that great things were about to happen when the sun and the moon appeared side by side in the sky. So they gazed this day as the sun and the moon stood side by side, and they wondered what was going to happen.

It was to mean more than anyone could imagine. Diana, the moon goddess, had insisted on meeting her brother, Apollo, the sun god. She yoked her milk-white stags to the silver moon chariot, and drove it across the sky. She reined up next to Apollo's sun chariot, whose red and gold, fire-maned stallions were pawing the air impatiently. They did not like to stop once they had started.

"Quickly, sister!" said Apollo. "We must go higher. If I halt my sun chariot too long in one place the earth will burn."

So, side by side, the sun and moon rose in the sky. Then brother and sister climbed out of their chariots and stood face to face.

"I know that this must be very important to you," said Apollo. "Otherwise you would not change the course of the sun and the moon."

"Important indeed," said Diana. "An evil thing is happening in the Eastern Kingdom. The son and daughter of the king are said to be radiantly beautiful. Cadmus and Europa are their names. And people have begun to whisper that this prince and princess are more beautiful than we are. Imagine! They dare compare these mortals to us!"

"Well," said Apollo. "We have managed such matters before. It seems to me we can handle this quite easily. You and I shall go there at twilight, when the sun and moon don't need us to drive them. With my golden arrows, I shall kill this Prince Cadmus. And you, with your silver arrows, will rid yourself of Princess Europa."

"Just what I had in mind!" cried Diana. "You always speak my thoughts, beloved twin. Let us go there this very evening."

"Agreed," said Apollo. "Now I must be on my

way. I have driven my chariot so high, that the earth is shivering this summer day."

Brother and sister parted. But they were not to meet at dusk for their deadly errand. As it happened, the West Wind had heard their conversation. Knowing that Zeus would be interested in their plans, he flew off to Mount Olympus to tell his story. When Zeus heard what the West Wind had to say, he grew very angry. He sent his messenger to summon the twins. Apollo and Diana stood before the throne of Zeus, who looked sternly down upon them and said, "Listen well and do not answer. Simply obey. I want no harm to come to Princess Europa or her brother, Cadmus. Know this, oh twins! I, your father, Zeus, have looked about the world from my place here on the mountain top. Wherever I looked I have found no one as beautiful or as good as the Princess Europa. I intend to make her my mortal bride. Man has grown slack and weak and cowardly. He is generally displeasing to me. I mean to breed a new race of heroes to lead mankind. And Europa will be my mortal wife. Do you understand?"

"Yes, Father," said Apollo.

"And you, Diana. Do you understand?"

"I understand, Father," said Diana. "And I shall obey you in all things."

"Go then, good children," said Zeus. "Off to

your tasks. Let the sun and moon ride the skies, bright with my favor."

Apollo and Diana hastened away, thankful that they had only been scolded by Zeus, not punished, for his anger was terrible.

Now on the eastern shore of the Inner Sea at that time, the grassland ran right down to the water. On this day, Europa and her friends were picking flowers and weaving them into garlands. She was a lovely, spirited, playful girl, and she took an enormous pride in being descended from mighty warriors. She loved tales of adventure, and admired courage beyond all things. On this summer morning, she wished she had something more exciting to do than weave garlands. Therefore, when a huge white bull suddenly appeared in the meadow and started browsing and the other girls shrank away, Europa cried out, "Oh, what a beautiful bull! What are you afraid of? If anyone dares me, I'll ride him!"

"No, princess!" cried her companions. "Don't try to ride him. He's too fierce."

"Fierce? Nonsense! Look at those big gentle brown eyes. Very well, if no one else dares to ride him, I will."

Then Europa seized a garland of flowers and ran toward the bull. Now she did not know it, but this bull was Zeus himself, who could take any form he desired. You see, it is very dangerous for the gods to appear before mortals in their godlike majesty and divine fire. Sometimes mortals are burned to cinders by this fire, and Zeus did not wish this to happen. Therefore, he changed himself into a white bull.

Europa wound the garland of flowers about the bull's horns, then leaped on his back and dug her heels into his side to make him gallop. He galloped through the meadow, past the meadow, through fields and groves. He did not even stop at the edge of the sea, but breasted the tide and swam away with Europa. Bull and rider vanished over the horizon. Europa tried to fight her fear, tried to bite back her sobs.

"Please," she said. "Swim back with me now. Take me back, please. Otherwise, my brother, Cadmus, will come hunting for you, and he will kill you."

But the bull kept swimming. It was a perfect day. Light danced on the waves. Europa sat comfortably on the bull's broad back, holding on to its horns. She stopped sobbing and began to enjoy the adventure. No girl, she thought to herself, had ever traveled so far, and no girl in the world would be able to match the tale she would have to tell when she finally returned to her father's court. But she never returned.

When her frightened companions ran back to the palace and gasped out their story, the king was furious. He raged and stormed. His son, Prince Cadmus, was even angrier. But he did not waste his time in a fit of temper. Within an hour he had called up a crew, rigged out his ship, and was sailing out to sea, determined to find his sister if he had to search every corner of the world.

Indeed, he searched the whole world over. He went as far as he could in every direction. He traveled to the very edge of the world in the east, where the people eat only tangerines and do everything as slowly as they can. They ride giant turtles and when they have races, the one who comes in last is the winner. When he asked these people if they had seen his sister, Europa, it took them several days to answer his question. But when they had finished answering he knew she had not been there.

He went as far as he could to the south where the sun chariot swings low over the scorched brown sand. Here the people's hair grows out of their heads in the shape of parasols to protect them from the white-hot spokes of the sun wheel. At night the stars flare like torches. Tempers sizzle in the heat, and men fight each other with curved knives. Several parasol-haired men attacked Cadmus with their knives when he asked about his sister, but he fought them off. His sword was a blade of light as he whirled it in the sun, cutting down his enemies like grass. They fled, leaving their wounded on the sand. One of them moaned, saying, "Do not kill me, bright prince, and I will answer your question."

"Answer, then," said Cadmus. "Have you seen my sister, Europa, a lovely girl, riding on the back of a white bull?"

"We have seen no such princess," said the man. "As for a bull, we don't even know what that is. There is no animal by that name in this part of the world."

Cadmus knew that the man was telling the truth, so he left the southern edge of the world, and traveled north as far as he could. It was so cold there that the people were dressed completely in furs. They even wore fur masks so that all you could see were their eyes. When they spoke, the words froze in the air and fell tinkling to the ground, breaking up into letters — and Cadmus had to read their answer. It was the same answer. "No. We have not seen your sister. We have not seen the white bull."

Then Cadmus traveled westward — to a completely unknown part of the world. He sailed to the edge of the earth, to its western rim. Here was the Garden of the Hesperides, where Hera's golden apple tree grew. There he saw an astounding sight. A giant, tall as a mountain, with white hair and a white beard, was holding the world on his shoulders. It was Atlas, punished by Zeus for making war against the gods. Atlas was forced to hold the earth and the sky on his shoulders until the end of time.

The apple nymphs who guarded Hera's golden apple tree were very pleased to see Cadmus. They did not often see strangers in that part of the world, and they made the prince welcome. They fed him fruit from the orchard, and they sang to him. But they too had the same answer: "We have not seen your sister, nor have we seen the white bull." But they had a piece of advice for him. "You will need more help than we can give," they told him. "This theft of your sister sounds like some high matter of the gods. You must go to someone very wise, someone who knows the plans of the gods and can read the future. You must go to the oracle at Delphi, and ask what you want to know."

Cadmus thanked the kindly nymphs and set sail once again, eastward. He came to the land of Greece. There, on the slope of a sacred mountain, stood the white marble temple to Apollo, called Delphi. In caves within the mountain dwelt the priestesses of Apollo. These wise women, called oracles, could sometimes read the future, if asked properly.

Cadmus went down into a cave and there found a woman so old that her skin looked like the bark of a tree. But her eyes were very bright. She sat on a three-legged stool holding a staff of hazelwood. Cadmus bowed to her and said, "Greetings, priestess. I am Cadmus, prince of the East. I seek my sister, the Princess Europa, who was carried away by a white bull. I have searched the four corners of the world and can find no trace of her. I come to you, priestess of Apollo, wisest of women, to ask your help."

The old woman peered into his face. Then she raised her staff and tapped sharply on the rock floor of the cave, crying,

Mountain, steam!
Send me my dream!

Steam hissed suddenly out of a crack in the floor, wrapping itself about Cadmus and the old woman. Cadmus kept perfectly still. When the steam cleared, he saw that the old woman was asleep. She mumbled something. He bent to hear. The words came more clearly:

Fear not for your sister's life.
A god has taken her as wife.

"What god, Mother?" cried Cadmus. "Which one?"

But the old woman spoke no more, and seemed to slip into a deeper sleep.

"God or mortal — no one steals my sister!" cried Cadmus. "If you will not tell me who, I shall search among the gods themselves!"

He slipped a golden band off his arm and tossed it into the lap of the old woman. Then he rushed out of the cave. Outside, in the April morning air, what had happened in the cave seemed like a dream. Yet Cadmus knew he must guide himself by the old woman's words.

"I've often heard," he said to himself, "that these soothsayers speak in rhymes and riddles. Her answer was in rhyme, but it seemed clear enough. No riddle there. A god has stolen my sister. Very well, I shall visit the gods."

He decided to visit Vulcan first. The god of fire had built himself a workshop inside a live volcano in Sicily. There Cadmus went. He climbed the mountain and descended into the smoky crater. The place was full of sooty shadows lit only by the red volcanic fires.

Cadmus stared in wonder at the fire god. He was so huge that he seemed to fill the great crater. His enormous span of shoulders and broad chest were knotted with muscle. He wore a leather apron and swung a hammer, the handle of which was the trunk of a tree. The head of the hammer was a single lump of iron larger than a boulder. Vulcan swung this gigantic sledge as if it were a tack hammer. He hobbled from forge to forge, for he was lame, looking over the work of the one-eyed Cyclopes who were his helpers.

Cadmus could hardly make his voice heard through the hammering and clanging. He leaped up on an anvil as Vulcan came near, and spoke into the god's ear!

"Oh, Vulcan," he said. "Mighty smith, god of mechanics and inventors, forgive me for interrupting your labors, but I have a question I must ask you. Were you the god who changed himself into a white bull and ran off with my sister, Princess Europa?"

Vulcan's great laugh was like the clanging of hammer on anvil. "What need have I for a mortal wife? I am married to Venus, the goddess of love herself. She is all the wife I want. I'll tell you what. Why don't you go question Neptune? This whole affair seems more in his style somehow."

"Thank you, great Vulcan. I go to seek Neptune."

"Before you go, I have some gifts for you. You're a bold one, and I admire courage. Here are some things you may find useful on your adventures — a helmet of beaten brass which no battle-axe can dent, though swung by a giant. And here is a shield of polished brass. No sword or spear can pierce it. And see, it is polished more brightly

than any mirror so that you can flash the sun in
your enemies' eyes, confusing them. And take
this. The first two gifts are for defense, but a hero
must go on the attack. Here is a sword of thrice-
tempered iron that can cut through armor as easily as shears through a piece of cloth. Watch this!"

Vulcan swung the sword and struck an anvil,
splitting it cleanly in two. "Farewell, Cadmus.
Proceed on your quest. Use my weapons well, for
it is my guess that the time is coming when you
will need them."

"Thank you again, lord of metal. I promise to
treat your beautiful weapons with the honor that
is their due."

Cadmus climbed out of the volcano, went down
to the shore, and gazed out upon the purple sea.
He wondered how he could sink to its depths
without drowning and find Neptune's castle.
Then he saw a wonderful thing — a boat made of
coral and pearl drawn by twelve dolphins who
were swimming so fast that the boat only
skimmed the top of the waves. In the boat stood a
tall green-clad figure wearing a crown of pearls,
carrying a three-pronged staff, called a trident,
made of bright gold. She was so tall and beautiful
that Cadmus knew she was a goddess. He fell on
his knees, crying, "Welcome to you, beautiful
goddess...whoever you are."

"Who I am is wife of Neptune and goddess of the sea," she answered.

"I must speak to your husband, goddess. I have a question to ask that he alone can answer.'

"I know your question, Cadmus. And I know the answer too."

Cadmus rose from his knees, and stared at Neptune's wife in surprise. She smiled, and her smile was like light over water. "Are you surprised that I recognize you, and know of your quest? Word gets around very quickly among the gods, my boy. There aren't many mortals bold enough to seek us out and question us."

"Tell me, goddess. Did your husband, Neptune, steal my sister?"

"The answer is no. He did not. It is true that he is a master of sea-change, and full of wild moods. He would be quite capable of changing himself into anything and stealing anyone, but he did not take your sister. That I know."

"Thank you for your courtesy and kindness, oh queen of the sea," said Cadmus. "Then I must seek my sister elsewhere."

"Try Mercury," said the sea queen. "He is god of thieves, you know, and quite apt to steal anything. Besides, he is also god of commerce, gamblers, travelers, as well as being the messenger god. He knows everyone's affairs. Even if he didn't take your sister, he might be able to tell you who did."

"Thank you again, beautiful goddess. And grant me this last favor. Allow me to paint your wonderful green eyes on the bow of my ship so that their beauty may outstare all peril."

"You are a well-spoken young man," said the goddess. "Paint my eyes on the bow of your ship. I shall look through them every now and again and assure you safe passage. Farewell."

The dolphins whirled the sea queen away in her little boat of coral and pearl, but Cadmus did not have to search for Mercury. The god found him. A huge shadow glided toward Cadmus across the beach. He looked up, expecting to see an eagle, but it was no eagle. It was a winged god who slid through the bright air and perched on a rock. A smiling young god, glittering with gold at head and ankles, and holding a golden staff entwined with golden serpents.

"You are Mercury," gasped Cadmus. "I was about to seek you."

"I know you were," said Mercury. "We gods know what's going on in the world, particularly when it concerns us. Besides, you have caused a great deal of talk on Olympus. Rare indeed is the mortal who dares to seek out the high gods and question them about their behavior. It is usually the other way around."

"I thank you for seeking me out," said Cadmus. "Tell me then, great Mercury, divine messenger, was it you who stole my sister, Europa, to take for your mortal wife?"

"No," said Mercury. "It was not I. I have no wife and I do not intend to get one — goddess, half-goddess, or mortal. I travel far, and must travel light."

"Thank you, lord of distances," said Cadmus. "Then I must seek elsewhere."

"No!" said Mercury. He had stopped smiling. His face was stern, and his voice cut like a whiplash. "No! You will question no more gods, Cadmus."

"I do not wish to quarrel with a god," said Cadmus. "But I must seek my sister until I find her."

"Listen to me," said Mercury. "You have been very busy among the gods. You have learned that neither Vulcan nor Neptune has kidnapped Europa. And you know that I did not steal your sister. So how many gods does that leave you?"

"Hades," said Cadmus. "But I shall not seek him in the underworld. I know in my heart that my sister is not among the dead. And there is Apollo."

"Do not question Apollo. He would grow very angry at such a question. He is the sun god and his anger scorches. If you seek Apollo, you will be a cinder before you get your question out. Besides, I can vouch for him, it was not Apollo. Now who does that leave among the gods?"

"But — " whispered Cadmus. And he stopped, unable to speak the mighty name.

"Exactly," said Mercury. "Zeus! Father Zeus, king of the gods, whom we ourselves dare not question."

"But was it he?" asked Cadmus. "Was it he who changed himself into a white bull and took my sister as mortal wife?"

"It was Zeus," said Mercury. "You have been honored above all human families, for your sister has become the mortal bride of Zeus. She dwells now on Crete, the most beautiful island in the world. She is the mother of three sons, who will become mighty kings. They will build great empires and become the fathers of warriors and heroes. Europa herself is very happy, and would not trade her life for any other. Do not seek her further. Do not try to visit her on Crete. That coast is guarded by a bronze sentinel as tall as a tree. On the command of Zeus, he hurls huge boulders at ships that sail too near. Perhaps in time you will see your sister again, but not yet."

Cadmus felt the hot tears running down his face. But they were tears of joy, for he knew that his sister was safe and happy. "Thank you, great

Mercury," he murmured. "Thank you, god of messages. I can return now to the East. My father is old, and I shall soon be king."

"No," said Mercury. "Your quest is not ended. You are part of the family whom Zeus loves. Your sister, Europa, has become the mother of kings. Her name will be given to the whole western part of the world. But you too are part of the plan. You must settle these new lands. If you have the courage and the strength and the wisdom, you will found a new kingdom, and build a great city. But first you will have to pass through the most dreadful peril that has ever been faced by mortal man."

"What must I do?" asked Cadmus, standing tall and proud before Mercury. "My heart is singing with joy and pride! If Zeus sends great perils to test me, so much the better. I can prove myself, and go on to whatever deeds he wishes me to perform."

"Bravely spoken, Cadmus," said Mercury. "Here is the first thing you must do:

Follow a cow...
Where she rests
Tell yourself *now*."

Before Cadmus could question him further, Mercury leaped into the air, ankle-wings whirring. He hovered a moment, saying:

If I wish to send you word,
I'll send a purple bird.

Then the god flashed off into the blue air. "Farewell," he cried. But he was so high now that his voice drifted down as a gull's cry.

Cadmus watched the speck of gold vanish from sight. When he turned, there to his surprise stood a beautiful brown cow with large amber eyes and small horns. The cow mooed musically, then ambled off. Cadmus followed as Mercury had directed. He understood nothing. He only knew that he must do as the god had said. All the rest of that day he followed the cow. She wandered away from the coast and moved inland at the same ambling pace, which let her cover great distances. Cadmus followed. He could not stop to eat or drink, he had to keep the cow in sight.

Night came on. "Surely," Cadmus thought, "she will stop now." But the cow did not stop. The stars hung low as torches, and it was easy to see the cow. She climbed a low hill, and went down the other side. Still Cadmus followed. His legs were weary. The helmet and shield and sword that Vulcan had given him seemed to weigh more with every step. They seemed to be dragging him down to the ground. But he could not cast off his weapons, nor could he rest as long as the cow moved before him. All night he followed her. Finally, he could walk no further. He fell to the ground.

"Am I to disappoint Zeus in my first test?" he said to himself. "Shall I fail simply because I am weary? No! This cannot be!"

Cadmus tried to drag himself to his feet, but he could not. So he crawled after the cow on his hands and knees. Fortunately, the cow seemed to be tiring and was going more slowly. She was climbing the slope of a steep hill, and that slowed her even more. Cadmus climbed the hill after her, dragging himself along on his knees, pulling himself on by the strength of his arms. Finally, the cow reached the top of the hill, and began to go down the other side. Now Cadmus simply let himself roll after her. When she started across the plain, he crawled after her. But now he had to crawl more slowly. His knees were scraped and bleeding. His hands were bleeding.

"I will go on even if my flesh is torn away and I have to creep on my bones," he said to himself.

Then to his delight, he saw the cow suddenly fold herself into a low shadow and lay down to rest. As he watched, the cow lowered her head and slept. Cadmus drew in a great breath of the fresh air. He took off his helmet, lay down his shield, and placed his sword carefully on it. Then he also slept.

When he awoke, the sun was high. The cow was gone, but it did not matter. Where she had rested there was a circle of crushed grass, and Cadmus suddenly knew what Mercury had meant. Here was where he must build his city. Indeed, it was a perfect site for a city. There was a broad plain, cut by two rivers and surrounded by low hills, offering natural defense against an enemy.

"I will build my city here!" cried Cadmus, turning his face to the sky. "Here will I found my kingdom!"

He gazed about the great empty plain. "But how can I even begin? Oh, well, Zeus said I must. And he who sent the task will send the tools."

Suddenly, the air was filled with a hideous clanking sound. The sun was blotted out by an enormous shadow. Cadmus looked up, and brave as he was, he almost fainted away with sheer terror. The sight that he saw was the most dreadful ever seen by man. Imagine an alligator as big as a ship — a flying alligator, with brass wings. This monster's entire hide was made of sliding brass scales, and it had a long thick tail bristling with brass spikes. Its feet had brass claws like baling hooks, but this was not the worst part. This beast, which was a dragon, spat flame from its mouth. Hot red fire spurted from its jaws.

The dragon was still a mile away, but Cadmus

felt the awful heat begin to roast him as he stood there on the plain. He knew that this was the peril of which Mercury had spoken. This was the monster he would have to destroy before he could build his city and found a kingdom. And Cadmus knew that there was no way under the morning sun that he could fight this flaming, spiked beast. The heat had become unbearable. Clutching his shield and sword, his helmet firmly planted on his head, Cadmus rushed to the river. He dived as deep as he could. His heavy weapons carried him to the bottom but, remembering a trick he had learned as a boy, Cadmus seized a handful of hollow reeds just before he dived.

He poked a reed up to the surface of the water, and held the other end in his mouth so that he could draw in enough air to keep himself alive. He felt the icy water grow warm as the dragon passed overhead. But the flames could not reach him. He waited, crouched on the bottom of the river until the clanging faded away. Then he climbed out of the river. He was covered with slimy mud, exhausted, and very downhearted. He knew that he must seek help.

"Good morning, Cadmus."

He whirled about, saw no one. Then he spotted a bird, flying in slow circles above his head.

"Was it you who spoke?" he said to the bird.

"I don't see anyone else here," said the bird.

"Since when do birds speak?"

"When they have been educated as I have. Then they learn to speak — quite well too."

The bird looked something like a crested blue-jay. And had the same kind of bossy voice. But instead of blue, it was purple. Then Cadmus remembered Mercury's last instruction.

> If I wish to send you word,
> I'll send a purple bird.

"Did Mercury send you?" cried Cadmus.

"He did, indeed. And he sent this message.

> To make the dragon yield,
> Let him dread his head
> Upon your shield."

And the bird flew away. "Wait!" cried Cadmus. "I don't understand."

"That's the entire message," said the bird. "Farewell."

The bird disappeared. Cadmus tried to puzzle out the meaning of the message. He knew that he did not have much time. In the distance he heard a tiny chiming, the brass scales clanking; the dragon was flying his way again.

"These rhymes and riddles spoken by gods and oracles seem to come true," he said to himself. "If only I could get the meaning of this one. But it's a puzzle, and I don't have much time."

To make the dragon yield,
Let him dread his head
Upon your shield.

"Well, I have a shield all right, but what does that have to do with the dragon's head?"

Cadmus had been wiping the muddy shield all this while with a handful of rushes. Now he studied it intensely. What he saw was his own face. The bright shield was a mirror.

"That's it!" he cried. "I understand! I must let the dragon see himself in the shield. But to do that he will have to get very close...much too close for comfort. Now may all the gods help me, for here he is!"

Indeed, the great shadow had darkened the plain again. The hot breath of the dragon was scorching the grass. Cadmus saw the dragon, jaws yawning, swooping toward him in a long curving dive. "He's stopped spouting flame," thought Cadmus. "He must want to eat me and doesn't want me over-cooked."

The dragon swooped low and struck at Cadmus with one great brass claw. Brass rang on brass as the claw struck the helmet Vulcan had made. But Cadmus was not touched; the claw did not pierce the helmet. The monster swerved in the air and flew back, flailing with his great tail. But Cadmus was ready. He sliced off the tip of the dragon's tail with the sword Vulcan had made. The beast howled in agony, rose to a great height, and came diving down, furiously beating his enormous wings and lashing his wounded tail. The dragon was falling with all his tremendous weight but Cadmus stood his ground. He looked up, and saw the terrible monster hurtling toward him — jaws open, teeth flashing like ivory daggers.

"Now is the time," he thought. "I must test Mercury's rhyme."

He held up the shield, stood with its bright brass disk covering his face and torso. The shield was on his bent left arm, his right arm held the sword. He stood rooted to the ground. He did not let his arm tremble, but held the shield steady as the dragon dove straight at him. The monster fell headfirst toward the shield, and on it saw a sight so horrible that it penetrated even that dim dragon brain. It was, of course, his own reflection in the mirror of the shield. But the dragon had never seen himself before and he did not know he was looking at himself. He thought another monster was attacking him. When he spit flame at the shield, he thought the monster facing him spit flame right back. When he saw this, the dragon gasped in horror.

Now when you gasp in horror you draw your breath in. That is what the dragon did. He drew in a great breath, not of air but of fire, for he was spitting flame at the time. He inhaled his own flame. Fire entered him and scorched everything inside. Lungs, liver, and heart were burned to a crisp. With a terrible choking shriek of agony the dragon fell to the plain. The fire had worked itself outward, and as Cadmus watched, the whole great length of the monster burned in a bright blue flame. The air was filled with bitter smoke, but it was sweet to Cadmus, seeing his enemy perish before his eyes. The dragon burned away completely, leaving only a handful of brass scales and his ivory teeth, for ivory does not burn.

In the thrashings of his last agony, the dragon had scorched and trampled the grass in a great circle so that it looked as if a city were being built.

"Thank you, Mercury!" cried Cadmus. "Thank you, great Zeus! You have sent my enemy and given me the courage to fight."

"Good work, Cadmus!" said a voice. "Mercury sends his congratulations." It was the purple bird again, circling slowly about Cadmus.

"I bid you welcome, purple bird. And thank you for your words of good advice."

"Mercury sends this last word to you, Cadmus," said the bird. "Listen well.

Set blade to earth and dig beneath
Then plant the dragon's teeth."

The bird flew off swiftly before Cadmus could question him further.

"Well, all the other riddle-rhymes worked," thought Cadmus. "No reason why this one shouldn't."

He picked up his sword and poked its point into the earth, to make a hole. Then he walked across the field, making a neat row of holes. When he finished one row, he began another, until he had a hundred holes, enough for the dragon's hundred teeth. He went to the pile of ivory and brass, all that was left of the dragon, and filled his helmet with the teeth. Then he went from hole to hole, planting a tooth in each, and carefully covering it over with earth. He planted fifty of the dragon's teeth in this way. But he had no time to plant the rest. Before his astounded eyes metal spikes came up out of the earth. As Cadmus watched, fifty armed men grew swiftly from the holes and stepped out on the field. Each of them wore a helmet, breastplate, shield, and either carried a sword or battle-axe. They were huge fierce-looking men. They glared about angrily, suspiciously, not knowing where they were. Cadmus ducked behind a rock. He had led men in battle, and he knew when men were in a killing mood.

"Fifty of them," he said to himself. "Too

many. I'll have to reduce that number."

Hiding behind the boulder, he threw out a stone. It struck the helmet of one man, who turned furiously on his neighbor and hit him with his axe, killing him. Then the man next to the man who had fallen attacked the first warrior. Then he was attacked immediately by two others. The fighting spread. Cadmus kept himself hidden behind the rock, occasionally throwing out another stone when he thought the fighting might stop. Cadmus let them fight until all but seven were killed. Then he sprang out of his hiding place, stood upon the rock, and raised his sword.

"Stop!" he shouted.

The men stopped fighting and gaped at him.

"I am your king. I am Cadmus. The gods have sent you here to this plain to help me build a city, and found a kingdom. You shall lead my armies."

But the men were not ready for such words. They were still full of anger. They charged Cadmus, who sprang off the rock, and met them head on. The helmet made by Vulcan could not be dented. The shield made by Vulcan could not be pierced. And the sword made by Vulcan sheared through the attackers' armor. Swiftly, he killed two of them. The others fell back.

"You see," he said. "It was meant to be. The gods protect me and the gods speak through me. I am your king. You are my captains. Now let us build our city."

They knelt then before Cadmus and swore to serve him faithfully. Under his direction, the five men built a city that was first called Cadmea and then called Thebes. Each of the five led an army that marched forth to conquer their enemies and make Thebes into a great kingdom. All that took years, of course. But it started on that bright morning when Cadmus held his ground and trusted his destiny.

Cadmus did not see his sister again. Years later, when Thebes had become a great kingdom, and Cadmus a great king, he married a beautiful goddess named Harmonia, daughter of Vulcan and Venus. The wedding of Cadmus and Harmonia was the first wedding of a mortal ever attended by the gods. They all came, and they all brought gifts. Europa came too. Brother and sister embraced again. And Europa ever after treasured the gift which her brother, Cadmus, gave her — an ivory necklace made of the dragon's teeth which Cadmus had not planted.

The Beautiful Witch

Ulysses was sailing home with three ships and a hundred men. But in the first two weeks at sea, he lost two ships and most of their crew. One ship was driven onto a reef by a sudden gale and wrecked completely. Another ship was stomped to splinters by angry giants who would not allow anyone to land on their island. As for the men, many drowned, many more were devoured by sea monsters and man-eating ogres.

Now, in his third week at sea, Ulysses was left with only one ship and a crew of thirty men. He was in an unknown part of the sea, among strange islands. He did not want to risk another landing.

But food and water were running low, and he knew he had to take the risk.

He moored his ship off a small, heavily wooded island, and ordered his men to wait on board until he signaled to them. He wanted to explore the island alone before disembarking his crew. Ulysses rowed toward shore in a small skiff, beached the boat and then struck inland. He climbed a low hill, then up a tree near the top of the hill. Now he was high enough for a clear view on all sides.

A feather of smoke, rising from a grove of trees, caught his eye. He climbed down and made his way toward the smoke. Glimmering through the trees, he saw what looked like a small castle of polished gray stone. He did not dare go near, for he could hear strange howling sounds. A pack of dogs, he thought, but they sounded unlike any dogs he had ever heard.

He left the grove, and made his way back toward the beach. He couldn't decide whether to sail away immediately or take a chance on having his men land. He didn't like the sound of that howling. There was something in it that chilled his bones. Still, he had no real choice. His men were hungry and the little island offered plenty of game to hunt and streams of pure water. So Ulysses signaled his men to come ashore on five small boats. When they landed on the beach, he divided them into two groups. One group he led himself. The other he assigned to his most trusted officer, Tyro. He ordered Tyro to scout the castle, and then, with his own party, left to explore the coastline.

As Tyro and his band of men approached the castle, they heard the strange howling. It grew louder as they approached. Some of the men drew their swords. Others notched arrows to their bow-strings as they pressed on preparing to fight. When they passed the last screen of trees and came to the walls of the shining gray castle, they saw a terrible sight. A pack of wolves and lions were running together, like hounds, racing around the walls.

When the animals caught sight of the men they flung themselves on the strangers. So swiftly did this happen that no man had time to use his weapon. The great beasts stood on their hind legs, put their forepaws on the men's shoulders, and licked their faces. They uttered low growling whines. Tyro, who was half-embracing a huge tawny lion, said, "These fearsome beasts greet us as though we were their lost friends. Look at their eyes. How sad they are — as if they were trying to tell us something."

Just then they heard someone singing in the

castle. It was a woman's voice, so lovely that without seeing her they knew the woman was beautiful.

Tyro ordered his men to go into the castle and then report back to him. "I will stay here and make sure you are not surprised," he said.

Tyro stood watch at the castle gate — sword in one hand, dagger in the other, and bow slung across his back. The rest of the men entered the castle. They followed the sound of singing through the rooms and out onto a sunny terrace. There a woman sat weaving. The bright flax leaped through her fingers as if it were dancing to the music in her voice. The men stood and stared. The sun seemed to be trapped in her hair — it was so bright. She wore a dress as blue as the summer sky, matching her eyes. Her long white arms were bare to the shoulders, and when she stood up and greeted them, they saw she was very tall.

"Welcome, strangers," she said. "I am Circe, daughter of Helios, a sun god. I can do magic — weave simple spells, and read dreams. But let us not talk about me, tell me about yourselves. You are warriors, I see, men of the sword. I welcome you. I shall have baths drawn for you and clean garments laid out. And then, I hope, you will all be my guests for dinner."

When Ulysses' men had bathed and changed,

Circe gave them each a red bowl, into which she put a kind of porridge made of cheese, barley, honey, and wine — and a few secret things known only to herself. The odor that arose from the food was more delicious than anything the men had ever smelled before. And as each man ate he felt himself doing strange greedy things — lapping, panting, grunting, and snuffling at the food. Circe passed among them, filling the bowls again and again. And the men, waiting for their bowls to be filled, looked about. Their faces were smeared with food. "How strange," they thought. "We're eating like pigs."

And as this thought came to the men, Circe passed among them, touching each one on the shoulder with a wand, saying,

> Glut and swink,
> Eat and drink,
> Gobble food and guzzle wine.
> Too rude I think for human folk,
> Quite right, I think,
> For *swine*!

As she said this spell in her lovely laughing voice, the men began to change. Their noses grew wide and long; their hair hardened into bristles; their hands and feet became hooves and they ran about on all fours, sobbing and snuffling, searching the floor for bones and crumbs.

But all the time they were crying real tears from their little red eyes, for they were pigs only in form. Their minds were still the minds of men, and they knew what had happened to them.

Circe kicked them away from the table. "Out! Out!" she cried, striking them with her wand and herding them out of the castle into a large sty. And there she flung them acorns and chestnuts and red berries, and watched them grubbing in the mud for the food she threw. She laughed a wild hard bright laugh and went back into the castle.

While all this was happening, Tyro was waiting at the gate. When the men did not return, he crept up to a bow-slit in the castle wall and looked in. It was dark now, and he saw the glimmer of torchlight and the dim shape of a woman at a loom, weaving. But he saw nothing of his men. And he could not hear their voices. A great fear seized him and he raced off as fast as he could, hoping that the beasts would not howl. The wolves and lions stood like statues or walked like shadows. Their eyes glittered in the cold moonlight, but none of them uttered a sound.

Tyro ran until the breath strangled in his throat. He thought his heart would crack out of his ribs, but he did not stop. He kept running, stumbling over roots, slipping on stones. He ran and ran until he reached the beach and fell into Ulysses' arms. He gasped out the story — told Ulysses of the lions and wolves, of the woman singing in the castle, and how the men had gone in and not come out.

Ulysses said to his men, "I must go to the castle to see what has happened, but there is no need for you to risk your lives. Stay here. If I do not return by sunset tomorrow, then you must board the ship and sail away, for you will know that I am dead."

The men pleaded with him not to go. But he said, "I have sworn an oath that I will never leave a man behind. If there is any way I can prevent this, I must. Farewell, dear friends."

It was dawn by the time Ulysses found himself among the oak trees near the castle and heard the first faint howling of the animals. As he walked through the rose and gray light, a figure started up before him. It was a slender youth in golden breastplate, golden hat, and golden sandals with golden wings on them. And he held a golden staff. Ulysses fell to his knees.

"Why do you kneel, sir?" said the youth. "You are older than I am, and a mighty warrior. You should not kneel."

"Ah," cried Ulysses. "Behind your youth I see time itself stretching to the beginning of things. I know you. You are Mercury, the swift one, the god of voyagers, the messenger god. I pray you have come with good tidings for me."

"I have come to warn you," said Mercury. "In that castle sits one who awaits you. Her name is Circe and she is a very dangerous person. A sorceress. A sea witch. A doer of magical mischief. And she is waiting for you, Ulysses. She sits at her loom, waiting. She has already bewitched your shipmates. She fed them, watched them make pigs of themselves, and finally helped them on their way. In short, they are now in a pig sty being fattened."

"I'm used to danger," said Ulysses. "I have faced giants and ogres but what can I do against magic?"

"I have come to help you," said Mercury. "Neptune's anger against you does not please all of us, you know. We gods have our moods but we must keep things in balance. Now listen closely...you must do exactly as I say..."

Mercury snapped his fingers and a flower appeared. It was white and very sweet-smelling, with a black and yellow root. He gave it to Ulysses.

"This flower is magical," said Mercury. "So long as you carry it, Circe's drugs will not work on you. Now go to the castle. She will greet you and feed you. You will eat the food, but it will not harm you. Then you must threaten to kill her. She will plead with you, and then try to enchant you with her voice, her face, her manner. You will not be able to resist them. No man can — nor any god either. And there is no counterspell that will work against her beauty."

"What chance do I have then?" said Ulysses.

"The chance you give yourself. If you want to see your home again, and rescue your men from the sty, you must resist her long enough to make her swear the great oath of the immortals. She must swear that she will not do you any harm as long as you are her guest. That is all I can do. The rest is up to you. Farewell."

The golden youth disappeared like a ray of sunlight. Ulysses shook his head, wondering whether he had really seen the god, or only imagined him. When he saw that he was still holding the curious flower, he knew that Mercury had indeed been there. So he marched on toward the castle, through the pack of lions and wolves, who leaped about him. They looked at him with their great intelligent eyes, trying to warn him in their snarling growling way. He stroked their heads as he passed among them, and went on into the castle.

And here he found Circe sitting at her loom, weaving and singing. She wore a white tunic and a flame-colored scarf, and was as beautiful as the dawn. She stood up and greeted him.

"Welcome, stranger."

"Thank you, beautiful lady."

"No. Thank *you*. I live here alone and seldom see anyone. I almost never have guests. So you are most welcome, great warrior. I know that you have seen battle and adventure, and have tales to tell."

Circe's servants drew Ulysses a warm, perfumed bath and gave him clean garments to wear. When he came back, Circe gave him a red bowl full of the same food she had given his men. Its fragrance was intoxicating. Ulysses wanted to plunge his face into the bowl and grub up the food like a pig. But he held the flower tightly, and kept control of himself. He ate slowly, and did not quite finish the food.

"Delicious," he said.

"Will you not finish?" she asked.

"I am not quite as hungry as I thought," Ulysses replied.

Circe turned her back to him as she poured the wine, and he knew she was putting a powder in it. He smiled to himself, then drank of the wine, and said, "Delicious. Your own grapes?"

"You look weary, stranger," she said. "Sit and talk with me."

"Gladly," said Ulysses. "We have much to talk about, you and I. I'm something of a farmer myself. I raise cattle on my own little island of Ithaca, where I'm king. Won't you show me your livestock?"

"Livestock? I keep no cattle here."

"Don't you? I thought I heard pigs squealing out there. I must have been mistaken."

"Yes," said Circe. "Badly mistaken."

"But you do have interesting animals. I was amazed by the wolves and lions outside your gates. They run in a pack like dogs — very friendly for such savage beasts."

"I taught them to be friendly," said Circe. "I'm friendly myself, and I like all the members of my household to share my good will."

"They have remarkable eyes," said Ulysses. "So big and sad and clever. You know, they looked to me like ... human eyes."

"Did they?" said Circe. "Well — the eyes go last."

Then she came to him swiftly, raised her wand, and touched him on the shoulder, saying: "Change, change, change! Turn, turn, turn!"

Nothing happened. Her eyes widened when she saw him sitting there unchanged, sniffing at the flower he had taken from his tunic. He took the wand from her and snapped it in two. Then he drew his sword, seized her by her long golden hair, and forced her to her knees.

"You have not asked me my name," he said. "It is Ulysses. I am an unlucky man, but not altogether helpless. You have changed my men into pigs. Now I will change you into a corpse."

Circe did not flinch before the sword. Her great blue eyes looked into his. "But I think living might be more interesting — now that I have met you," she murmured.

Ulysses tried to turn his head, but he sank deeper into the blueness of her eyes.

"Yes, I am a sorceress," she whispered. "A witch. But you are a sorcerer too, are you not? You have changed me more than I have changed your men. I changed only their bodies, you have changed my soul. It is no longer a wicked plotting soul, but soft and tender — full of love for you."

"Listen to me, beautiful witch. Before there can be any love between us, I must ask you to swear the great oath that you will not harm me in any way as long as I am your guest. You must swear not to wound me or suck away my blood, as witches do, but treat me honestly. And that, first of all, you will restore my men to their own forms, and let me take them with me when I leave."

"Don't speak of leaving," said Circe softly.

Circe swore the oath. She took Ulysses out to the sty, and as the pigs streamed past her, rushing to Ulysses, she touched each one on the shoulder with her wand, muttering:

Snuffle and groan,
Gasp and pant.
Muffle your moan,
I dis-enchant.

For your captain fine
I undo my deed,
And release you swine
As agreed.

As she spoke the spell, each pig stood up. His hind legs grew longer, his front hooves became hands. His eyes grew, his nose shrank, and his quills softened into hair. Each was himself once more, with his own form, his own face, but taller now and younger. The men crowded around Ulysses, shouting and laughing.

"Welcome, my friends," he said. "You have gone a short but ugly voyage to the animal state. You have returned looking very well, but it is clear that we are in a place of strong magic and must conduct ourselves with care. Our enchanting hostess, Circe, has become so fond of our company that she insists we stay a while longer. But I don't think we can accept the lady's hospitality."

Circe seized Ulysses by the arm, and drew him away from the others.

"You don't understand," she said. "I don't want you as a guest. I want you to be my husband."

"I am much obliged, dear lady. But I am already married."

"Only to a mortal. That doesn't count. I am a goddess — an immortal. We can have as many husbands as we like."

"How many have you had?" cried Ulysses.

"Ah, don't say it like that," said Circe. "I have been a widow quite often, it is true. But please understand. I am immortal. I cannot die. I have lived since the beginning of things."

"How many husbands have you buried, dear widow?"

"I do not let them die," replied Circe. "I cannot bear dead things — especially if they are things I have loved. I turn them into animals, and they roam this beautiful island forever."

"That explains the wolves and lions outside the walls then," said Ulysses.

"Ah, they are only the best!" cried Circe. "The mightiest warriors of ages gone. I have had lesser husbands. They are now rabbits, squirrels, boars, cats, spiders, frogs — and snails. See that little monkey on the wall trying to pelt us with walnuts? He was very jealous, very bossy and jealous and still is. I pick their animal forms to match their dispositions, you see. Isn't that thoughtful of me?"

"Tell me," said Ulysses. "When you tire of me,

will I be good enough to join the lions and wolves — or will I be something less? A toad, perhaps, or a snail?"

"A fox, of course," said Circe. "With your red hair and your swiftness and your cunning ways — oh, yes, a fox. You are the only man who has ever withstood my spells, Ulysses. I beg you, stay with me."

"I have told you I cannot."

"I can teach you to wipe out of your mind all thoughts of home, all dreams of battle and voyage. And I will do for you what I have done for no other mortal. I will teach you to live forever. Yes, I can do that, Ulysses. We can live together always, and never grow old."

"Can such a thing be?" whispered Ulysses whose one fear in the world was of growing too old for voyages and adventure. "Can you actually keep me from growing old?"

"I can," said Circe. "If you want me to. The decision is yours. You can stay here with me, and make this island your home. Or you can resume your voyage and meet dangers more dreadful than any you have yet seen. You will encounter sea monsters and land monsters, giant cannibals and rocks that will try to crush your ship between them. Neptune's anger will grow each day. If you leave this island, Ulysses, you will see your friends die before your eyes. Your own life will be imperiled a thousand times. You will be battered, bruised, torn, wave-tossed — all this if you leave me. It is for you to decide."

Ulysses stood up and walked to the edge of the terrace. He could see the light dancing on the blue water. He could hear the wolves and lions beyond the wall. Near the empty sties, he saw his men, healthy and tanned. Some were wrestling, some were practicing with spears and bows. Circe had crossed to her loom and was weaving. He thought of his wife at home in Ithaca when she would sit and weave. Her hair was not the color of burning gold. It was black. And she was much smaller than Circe, and did not sing. Certainly she was no goddess. She was very human, and did not have the power to keep him young forever. He went to Circe.

"I have decided," he said. "I must go."

"Must you?"

"Yes."

"I have read the future for you, Ulysses. You know what lies in store for you if you leave this place. When disaster strikes, remember that the choice was yours."

"I am a voyager, Circe. And danger is my destiny. Toil. Battle. Uncertainty. That is my destiny, and the nature of voyages."

"Go quickly, then! If you stay here any longer I shall break my oath. I shall keep you here by force and never let you go."

Ulysses left the castle at once and called to his men. He led them back to the beach where they arrived just before sunset. They piled into the skiffs and pushed off for the anchored ship. They stepped the mast, rigged the sails, and scudded away. They caught a northwest wind. The sails filled, and the black ship ran out of the harbor. Ulysses' face was wet with Circe's tears, and his heart was heavy. But then the salt spray dashed into his face, and he laughed.

The lions and wolves had followed the men down to the beach, and stood breast-deep in the surf. They gazed after the white sail. Their lonesome howling was the last sound the men heard as the ship ran for the open sea.

Keeper of the Winds

For three sunny days the black ship sped southward from Circe's island. Ulysses began to hope that Neptune's anger had cooled enough to allow fair sailing the rest of the way home. He took the helm himself, and kept it night and day, although his sailors pleaded with him to take some rest. But he was wild with longing to get home to his wife and young son, and the dear land of Ithaca that he had not seen for many years.

At the end of the third night, just as the first light of day was staining the sky, Ulysses saw something very strange. At first he thought it was a trick of the light, and he rubbed his eyes and looked again. But there it was, a towering bright wall of beaten bronze floating on the sea and blocking their way.

"Well," he thought to himself. "It cannot stretch across the sea. There must be a way around it."

He began to sail along the wall, trying to find his way around it. Ulysses had no way of knowing this, but the vengeful sea god had guided his ship to the island fortress of Aeolus, keeper of the winds.

When the world was very new, the gods had become wary of the terrible strength of the winds, and had decided to tame them. Zeus and Neptune, working together, had floated an island out onto the sea, and then encircled it with a mighty bronze wall. Then they raised a mountain on the island, and hollowed it out until it became a huge stone dungeon. Into this hollow mountain they stuffed the struggling winds, and made Aeolus their jailer. Whenever the gods wanted to stir up a storm and needed a certain wind, they sent word to Aeolus. He would draw his sword and stab the side of the mountain, making a hole big enough for the wind to fly through. If the North Wind were wanted, he stabbed the north side of the mountain. For the East Wind he stabbed the east slope, and so on. When the storm was done,

Aelous would whistle the wind home again. Then the huge brawling gale would crawl back whimpering to its hole.

Aeolus was an enormously fat little god with a long wind-tangled beard and a red wind-beaten face. He loved to eat and drink, play games, and hear stories. He had twelve children, six boys and six girls. He sent them out one by one to ride the back of the wind and manage the weather for each month.

It happened that just as Ulysses was sailing southward, Aeolus decided to punish his winds. On a night of mischief they had howled around his castle, shattering the great crystal windows, lifting the tiles from the roof, and uprooting a thousand-year-old oak that was his pride. "Break my windows, would you?" bellowed Aeolus. "Blow the cows into the next field and uproot my beautiful oak—very funny. Well, you'll bake in your mountain until I cook the mischief out of you!" And with this he hurled the winds headlong into their prison cave.

Since the winds were walled up, a great calm fell upon the seas just as Ulysses was trying to find a way around the bronze wall. The water was oily and still. The ship's sail drooped. They were becalmed. For a day and a night the ship bobbed on the water waiting for a breeze. Ulysses stared helplessly at the bronze wall towering before him. Food and water were running desperately low.

"All right, men!" Ulysses shouted. "Haul sail! Out oars! We must row for it!"

The men bent to the oars and the ship crawled around the bronze wall. Finally they came to a huge gate. As Ulysses gazed upon it in amazement, the gate swung open. The water ruffled darkly, and a gale struck. The shrouds snapped, the sails bulged, the mast groaned, and the ship was blown through the gate, which immediately shut behind them. Once within the wall, the wind fell off, and Ulysses found his ship drifting toward a beautiful hilly island. Suddenly there was another great howling of wind. The sun was blown out like a candle. Darkness fell. Ulysses felt the deck leap beneath him as the ship was lifted halfway out of the water and hurled through the blackness. He tried to shout, but the breath was torn from his mouth and he was thrown to the deck, unconscious.

When they finally awoke, Ulysses and his men found themselves in the great castle of Aeolus. Invisible hands held torches for them, guided them to their baths, and gave them fresh clothing. Then the floating torches led them to the dining hall, where they were greeted by Aeolus and his twelve handsome children. A mighty banquet was laid before them, and they ate like starved men.

Finally Aeolus spoke: "Strangers, you are my guests. Uninvited, but guests all the same. By the look of you, you have had more than your share of adventures and should have fine stories to tell. I love a story full of fighting and danger and tricks. If you have any to tell then I shall entertain you royally. But if you are the kind of men who use your mouths only to stuff food into, then you are apt to find things a little unpleasant..."

"You, captain!" Aeolus roared, pointing at Ulysses. "You, sir. I take you to be the leader of this ragged crew. Do you have a story to tell?"

"For those who know how to listen, I have a tale to tell," said Ulysses.

"Your name?"

"Ulysses — of Ithaca."

"Mmm...yes," said Aeolus. "I seem to remember that name. Near Troy I think it was...a little quarrel. Yes...were you there?"

"I was there, dear host, and indeed took part in that petty quarrel that will be remembered by men when this island, and you and yours have vanished under the sea and been forgotten for a thousand years. I am Ulysses. My comrades before Troy were very mighty heroes, and in modesty I did no less than they."

"Yes," said Aeolus. "You are bold enough. Too bold for your own good, perhaps. But you have caught my attention. Tell on, captain."

Then Ulysses told of the Trojan War — of the great battles, the attacks and retreats, the hand-to-hand fighting. He told of friends and enemies. Of men killing and dying. Of heroes and cowards, and those in between.

Then he told of his own great trick which had ended the war. How he had made a hollow wooden horse of enormous size, and how the Greek army had hidden in the belly of the horse. He told how the Trojans, amazed by this gigantic statue, had dragged the horse inside their gates, and how the Greek warriors had crept out at night and taken the city and killed the Trojans.

Aeolus shouted with laughter. His face blazed and his body shook. "Ah, that's a trick after my own heart!" he cried. "You're a sharp one, you are. I knew you had a foxy look about you with that red hair and red beard. Wooden horse...ho ho....But tell me, is it true what they say about Troy? Was it a rich city?"

"Quite true," said Ulysses. "It was a wonderfully rich city."

"And you sacked it," Aeolus said. "You must be sailing home with a pretty piece of loot under your deck, eh?"

Ulysses smiled to himself. From his first glimpse of Aeolus he had recognized the wind god's greed, and he was prepared now to use it to his own advantage. "Yes," said Ulysses. "There was some very pleasant looting at Troy. I picked up this little curio in the royal palace — in the king's own chamber."

Ulysses opened a soft leather pouch at his belt, took something from it, and handed it to Aeolus.

"What is it?" asked Aeolus. "It looks like a frog made of green stone."

"That frog," said Ulysses, "is the largest emerald in the world."

"Is it, indeed?" murmured Aeolus. "Largest in the world, eh? Interesting..."

"More interesting than you think. Its jaw is hinged. See? Now ask it a question."

"You want me to question this toy? Foolishness!"

"Try it and see," said Ulysses. "I'll tell you this. It was made by Vulcan himself who can do some very ingenious things, as you know. Go ahead, ask it a question. Any question."

"Very well," said Aeolus. "Frog, frog, answer true — the strongest god is — who?"

"You," said the frog.

"Me?"

"You." And then the frog sang,

Gods they come,
Gods they go,
But the winds of Aeolus
Always blow...
Blowing late and soon
They quench the moon—
Gentle breeze
And wild typhoon...

"A marvelous song!" cried Aeolus. "Well sung too!"

"Know this, oh Aeolus," said the frog. "The earth was born when a wind, blowing starfire upon starfire, shaped it into a flaming ball. And the earth will die when foolish men — wise in evil — will hurl that flame upon each other. They will start a blaze that will turn the seas to steam and the mountains to cinder. And you alone will be left, Aeolus, master of winds, the last god."

"A most remarkable frog!" roared Aeolus. "A wise and musical frog, Ulysses. Truly a fine piece of booty to take from Troy."

"It is yours, Aeolus."

"Mine?"

"Yours, dear host," said Ulysses. "A slight return for your hospitality."

"By the gods, this is most generous of you, captain. In return you may have any favor within my power. Speak out, Ulysses. Ask what you will."

"There is only one thing I seek, great Aeolus. Your help. I need your help in getting home. It has been a long time since we saw our homes and families. We thirst for the sight of Ithaca."

"No one can help you better than I," Aeolus assured him. "You sail on ships, and I am keeper of the winds. Come with me."

He led Ulysses into the night. A hot orange moon rode low in the sky so they could see without torches. Aeolus led Ulysses to the mountain. He was carrying a sword in one hand and a great leather bag in the other. "Stand back," said Aeolus. "They come out with a rush."

"Who does?"

"The winds, man, the winds," said Aeolus. "They hate to be penned in that mountain. They are like caged beasts, but wilder and stronger than all the beasts in the world combined. They want to run free over land and sea, kicking up storms. But I alone can set them free. And let me tell you, friend, you are the first mortal ever to be granted use of the winds."

"I thank you, Aeolus."

"They are a tricky loan, though, these winds. They could mean your death unless you do whatever I tell you."

"I will do whatever you say," Ulysses promised.

"Stand back, then."

Ulysses stepped back as Aeolus stood tall before the mountain, chanting,

>Winds, winds, sally forth —
>South and East and surly North.
>Hurry, hurry, do not lag —
>Get inside this leather bag.

Then Aeolus stabbed the side of the mountain. There was a rushing, sobbing sound. He clapped the leather bag over the hole and Ulysses, amazed, saw the great bag flutter and fill. Aeolus held it closed, strode to the east face of the mountain and stabbed again. As the East Wind rushed out, he caught it in the sack. Then very carefully he wound a silver wire about the neck of the sack. It was full now, swollen, tugging at his arm like a huge leather balloon trying to fly away.

"In this bag," said Aeolus, "are the North Wind, the South Wind, and the East Wind —"

"What of the West Wind?" said Ulysses.

"He's for sailing." Aeolus strode now to the west slope of the mountain and chanted,

>Hurry now from stony lair,
>Wind that blows when sky is fair —
>Of all my winds the very best,
>Sailors' friend, the wind called West.

"But if the West Wind will bear me home," said Ulysses, "why do I need the other winds in the bag?"

"Need, indeed," said Aeolus. "You of all people should know how changeable the sea can be. In this bag are the three winds, North, South, and East, and you must keep them prisoner. But if you wish to change course — if a pirate should chase you, say, or a sea monster, or if an adventure beckons — then you open the bag very carefully, you and you alone, captain, and call up the wind you wish. Let just a breath of it out, then close the bag quickly and tie it tight. Winds grow swiftly, that is their secret. So they must be carefully guarded."

"I shall not change course," said Ulysses. "No matter what danger threatens or what adventure calls, I will sail straight for Ithaca. I shall not open your bag of winds."

"Good," said Aeolus. "But just in case, tie it to the mast, and guard it yourself. Let none of your men approach, lest they open it accidentally. And I will send the gentle West Wind to follow your ship and fill your sails and take you home. When you are safely home, then you can open the bag and I will call the winds home."

"Thank you, great Aeolus. Thank you, kindly Keeper of the Winds. I know now that the gods have answered my prayers. I shall be able to cease this weary heartbreaking drift over the face of the sea. I shall never stop thanking you, Aeolus, till the day I die."

"May that sad day be far off," said Aeolus politely. "Now, sir, much as I like your company, you had better gather your men and be off. I shall be uneasy until my winds return to me and I can shut them in the mountain again."

Ulysses went back to the castle and called his men together. Gladly they trooped down to the ship and went aboard. Ulysses bound the great leather sack to the mast, warning his men that no one must touch it on pain of death. Then he himself, armed with his sword, stood under the mast, guarding the sack.

"Up anchor!" he cried.

The West Wind rolled off the mountain and filled their sails. The black ship slipped out of the harbor, away from the island toward the wall of bronze. When they reached the wall, the great gate swung open and they sailed eastward over water oily with moonlight. Eastward they sailed for nine days and nine nights. In perfect weather they skimmed along, the West Wind hovering behind them, filling their sails, pushing them steadily home.

And for nine nights and nine days, Ulysses did not sleep. He did not close his eyes or sheathe his sword. He kept his station under the mast and had food and drink brought to him there. He never, for an instant, stopped guarding the sack.

Then on the morning of the tenth day, he heard the lookout cry, "Land ho!" Ulysses strained his eyes to see. What he saw made his heart swell. Tears ran down his face, but they were tears of joy. For he saw the dear familiar hills of home. He saw the brown fields of Ithaca, the twisted olive trees. And as he watched, he saw the white marble columns of his own palace on the cliff. And his men saw the smoke rising from their own chimneys.

When Ulysses saw the white columns of his palace, he knew that unless the West Wind failed, they would be home in an hour. And the friendly wind was blowing as steadily as ever. Ulysses heaved a great sigh. "I thank you, gods," he whispered. The terrible responsibility that had kept him awake for nine days and nights was over. He put up his sword, raised his arms, and yawned. Then he leaned against the mast, just for a moment.

Two of the men, standing in the bow, saw him slump at the foot of the mast, fast asleep. Their eyes slid up the mast to the great leather bag, plump as a balloon, straining against its bonds as the impatient winds wrestled inside.

And now it was that Neptune, swimming invisibly alongside the ship, saw the chance he had been waiting for. He clinked the heavy golden bracelets on his arms.

He heard one man say to the other, "Do you hear that? Those are coins, heavy golden coins clinking against each other. There must be a fortune in that sack."

"Yes," said the other man. "A fortune that should belong to all of us by rights. We shared the dangers and should share the booty."

"He has always been generous," said the first. "He shared the spoils of Troy."

"Yes, but that was then. Why doesn't he divide this great sack of treasure? Aeolus gave it to him, and we know how rich Aeolus is. He gave it to him as a guest gift, and he should share it."

"He never will. Whatever is in that bag, he does not want us to know about it. He has been guarding it all these nights and days, standing there always under the mast, eating and drinking where he stands. He never put up his sword."

"It is in its sheath now," said the second sailor. "And his eyes are closed. Look, he sleeps like a baby. I doubt that anything would wake him."

"What are you doing? What are you going to do with that knife? Are you out of your mind?"

"Yes, out of my mind with curiosity. Out of my mind with gold fever, if you must know. I mean to see what is in that bag."

"Wait — I'll help you. But you must give me half."

"Come then."

Swiftly and silently the two barefooted sailors padded to the mast. They slashed the rope that held the bag to the spar, and carried it away.

"Hurry — open it!"

"I can't. The wire's twisted in a strange knot. Perhaps a magic knot. I can't untie it."

"Then we'll do it this way!" cried the sailor with the knife, and he slashed at the leather bag. He was immediately lifted off his feet and blown like a leaf into the sea. The winds rushed howling out of the bag. They began to chase each other around the ship, screaming and laughing, jeering and growling and leaping, reveling in their freedom, roaring and squabbling, screeching around and around the ship. They fell on their gentle brother, the West Wind, and cuffed him mercilessly until he fled. Then they chased each other around the ship again, spinning it like a cork in a whirlpool.

When they heard the far faint whistle of the Keeper of the Winds, they snarled with rage and roared homeward to the isle of the winds, far to the west of Ithaca. As they rushed away, they snatched the ship along with them, ripping its sail to shreds, snapping its mast like a twig, and hurling the splintered hull westward over the boiling sea.

Ulysses awoke from his sleep to find the blue sky black with clouds, and his home dropping far astern. He saw his crew flung about the deck like dolls, and he saw the tattered sails and the broken spars, and he did not know whether he was asleep or awake. Was this some frightful nightmare, or was he awake now and asleep before, dreaming a fair dream of home?

With the unleashed winds screaming behind them at gale force, the trip back to Aeolus' island took them only two days. Once again the black ship was hurled onto the island of the winds. Ulysses left his crew and went to the castle. He found Aeolus in his throne room, and he stood before him, bruised, bloody, clothes torn, eyes like ashes.

"What happened?" cried Aeolus. "Why have you come back?"

"I was betrayed," said Ulysses. "Betrayed by sleep — the most cruel sleep of my life — and by a wicked, foolish, greedy crew who let the winds escape. We were snatched back from happiness even as we saw the smoke rising from our own chimneys."

"I warned you," said Aeolus. "I warned you not to let anyone touch that bag."

"And you were right, a thousand times right!" cried Ulysses. "Be generous once again. You can heal my woes, you alone. Renew your gift. Lend me the West Wind to bear me home again and I swear to you that I shall do everything you bid."

"I can't help you," said Aeolus. "No one can help whom the gods hate. And Neptune hates you. What you call bad luck is his hatred. And bad luck is very catching. So please go. Get on your ship and sail away from this island, and never return."

"Farewell," said Ulysses, and strode away.

He gathered his weary men and made them board the ship again. The winds were penned up in their mountain. The sea was sluggish. A heavy calm lay over the harbor. The crew had to row on their broken stumps of oars, crawling like beetles over the gray water. They rowed away from the island, through the bronze gate, and out upon the sullen sea.

Ulysses, heartbroken, almost dead of grief, tried to hide his feelings from the men. He stood on deck, barking orders, making them mend sail, patch hull, rig new spars, and keep rowing. He took the helm himself, and swung the tiller, pointing the bow eastward toward home, which once again lay at the other end of the sea.

Cupid and Psyche

There was a king who had three daughters. The youngest, named Psyche, was the most beautiful. She was so lovely, in fact, that kings and princes and warriors from all the countries around poured into her father's castle to ask for her hand in marriage.

"If we don't marry that girl off," the king said to his wife, "I'll have a war on my hands. But what are we going to do about her sisters?"

It was the custom, at that time, that daughters be married in the order of their age — the oldest one first, then the next oldest, and so on down to the youngest.

"We'll just have to break the rule," said the

queen. "The palace grounds are beginning to look like a battlefield. They're killing each other and trampling my peonies. I'll speak to her tonight."

But Psyche was not ready to get married. She was a kind girl and did not wish to make her sisters more jealous than they already were. Besides, there was no one she wanted to marry. She went off by herself to a grove in the woods, and there whispered a prayer to Cupid.

"Oh, archer of love," she said. "Please do this for me. Aim your golden arrows at two of those who seek to marry me. But make them love my sisters instead."

Cupid thought this the oddest prayer he had ever heard.

"It's usually the other way around," he said to himself. "The girl who prays to me usually wants me to help her *steal* her sister's suitor. This Psyche must be the most unselfish girl in the world."

Cupid was so curious about Psyche that he flew down to take a look for himself. When he saw her, it was just as though he had scratched himself with one of his own arrows. He hovered invisibly in the air above the grove where Psyche was praying. He began to feel the sweet poison spread in his veins, and he grew dizzy with joy and strangeness. Cupid had spread love, but never felt it. He had shot others, but never been wounded himself. He did not know himself this way.

He immediately flew to the castle, and just as Psyche's sisters were coming into the courtyard, he aimed his golden arrows at the first two suitors he saw. That very evening the king and queen were delighted to receive offers of marriage for their two eldest daughters.

"Now Psyche can marry," they said to each other joyfully. "And peace will return to the kingdom." Peace came, but not in the way they expected.

Cupid did not want anyone to court Psyche. He cast an invisible hedge of thorns around the girl so that no suitor could come near. Psyche welcomed being alone. No man or boy she had ever met matched her secret idea of what a husband should be. Now, behind the hedge of thorns, she could dream about him.

But the king and queen were very troubled. They could not understand why no one was asking to marry their most beautiful daughter. They understood even less why she didn't seem to care. They went to an oracle, who said:

"Psyche is not meant for mortal man. She is to be the bride of the one who lives on the mountain and conquers both man and god. Take her to the mountain, and say farewell."

When the king and queen heard this they thought their daughter was meant for some monster. They feared that she would be devoured, as so many other princesses had been devoured, to feed the mysterious appetite of evil. But they had to obey the oracle, and so they dressed Psyche in bridal garments, hung her with jewels, and led her to the mountain. The whole court followed, mourning as though it were a funeral instead of a wedding.

Psyche herself did not weep, but had a strange dreaming look on her face. She spoke no word of fear, wept no tear, as she kissed her mother and father good-bye. She stood tall on the mountain, her white bridal gown blowing about her, her arms full of flowers.

Soon the wedding party returned to the castle. When the last sound of their voices faded, Psyche stood alone listening to a great silence. Then the wind blew so hard that her hair came loose. Her gown was whipped about her like a flag and she felt a great pressure that she did not understand. She heard the wind itself whispering in her ear, saying: "Fear not, princess. I am the West Wind, the groom's messenger. I have come to take you home."

Psyche listened to the wind and believed what she heard. She was not afraid, even though she felt herself being lifted off the mountain and carried through the air like a leaf. She felt herself gliding down steps of air. She was carried through the failing light, through purple clumps of dusk, toward another castle, gleaming like silver on a hilltop. She was set down gently within the courtyard. It was empty, and there were no sentries, no dogs, nothing but shadows and the moon-pale stones of the castle. A carpet unreeled itself and rolled out to her feet. She walked over the carpet and through the doors. They closed behind her.

A torch burned in the air and floated in front of her. She followed it. It led her through a great hallway into a room. The torch whirled. Three more torches whirled in to join it, then stuck themselves in the wall and burned there, lighting the room. It was a smaller room, beautifully furnished. Psyche stepped onto the terrace which looked out over the valley toward the moonlit sea.

A table floated into the room, and set itself down solidly on its three legs. A chair placed itself at the table. Invisible hands began to set the table with dishes of gold and goblets of crystal. Food appeared on the plates, and the goblets were filled with purple wine.

"Why can't I see you?" she cried to the invisible servants.

A courteous voice said, "It is so ordered."

"And my husband? Where is he?"

"Journeying far. Coming near. I must say no more."

Psyche was very hungry after her windy ride, and she finished the delicious meal. The torch then led her out of the room to another room that was an indoor pool full of fragrant warm water. After she bathed herself, fleecy towels were offered to her, and a flask of perfume that smelled like a summer garden at dawn. Then Psyche went back to her room, and awaited her husband.

Presently she heard a voice in the room. A powerful voice speaking very softly, so softly that the words were like her own thoughts.

"You are Psyche. I am your husband. You are the most beautiful girl in the world, beautiful enough to make the goddess of love herself grow jealous."

Psyche could not see anyone. She felt the voice press hummingly upon her as if she were in the center of a huge bell.

"Where are you?"

"Here."

Psyche reached out her arms and heard the voice speak again. "Welcome home."

When she awoke next morning, Psyche was alone, but she was so happy she didn't care. She went dancing from room to room, exploring the castle, singing as she went. She explored the courtyard, and the woods nearby as well, and found only one living creature — a silvery greyhound, dainty as a squirrel and fierce as a panther. Psyche knew it was hers. The greyhound went exploring the woods with her, and showed her how he could outrace the deer. Psyche laughed with joy to see him run.

At the end of the day she returned to the castle. Her meal was served by the same invisible servants. She again bathed and put on fresh clothes. At midnight her husband came to her again, and she wondered how it was that of all the girls in the world she had been chosen to live in this magical place.

Day after day went by like this, and night after night. And each night he asked her, "Are you happy, lovely girl?"

"Yes, but I want to see you. I know you are beautiful, but I want to see for myself."

"That will be, but not yet. It is not yet time!"

"Whatever you say, dear heart. But then, can you not stay with me by day as well, invisible or not?"

"That too will change, perhaps. But not yet. It is too soon."

"But the day grows so long without you."

"You are lonely. You want company. Would you like your sisters to visit you?"

"My sisters! I had almost forgotten them. How strange."

"Shall I send for them?"

"I don't really care. It is you I want. I want to see you."

"You may expect your sisters tomorrow."

The next day the West Wind bore Psyche's two sisters to the castle, and set them down in the courtyard, windblown and bewildered. They were fearful, having been snatched away from their own gardens, but were relieved to find themselves floating so gently to this strange courtyard. How amazed they were then to see their own sister, whom they thought long dead, running out of the strange castle. She was more beautiful than ever — blooming with happiness, and more richly garbed than any queen. Psyche swept her sisters into her arms. She embraced and kissed them, and made them greatly welcome.

Then she led them inside. The invisible servants bathed them and helped them dress, then served them a delicious meal. With every new wonder they saw, with every treasure their sister showed them, they grew more and more jealous. They, too, had married kings, but little local ones. This castle made theirs look like dog kennels. They did not eat off golden plates and drink out of jeweled goblets. And their servants were the plain old visible kind. As they ate and drank, with huge appetites, they grew more and more displeased with every bite.

"Where is your husband?" asked the eldest sister. "Why is he not here to welcome us? Perhaps he didn't want us to come?"

"Oh, yes he did," cried Psyche. "It was his idea. He sent his servant, the West Wind, for you."

"Oho," sniffed the second sister. "So he's the one we have to thank for being taken by force and hurled through the air. A rough way to travel."

"But so swift," said Psyche. "Don't you like riding the wind? I love it."

"Yes, you seem to have changed in many ways," said the eldest. "But you're still not telling us where your husband is. It is odd that he doesn't want to meet us — very odd."

"Not odd at all," said Psyche. "He — he is rarely here by day. He — has things to do."

"What sort of things?"

"Oh, you know. Wars, peace treaties, hunting...you know the things men do."

"Is he often away then?"

"Oh, no. That is, only by day. At night he returns."

"Ah, then we shall meet him tonight. At dinner, perhaps."

"No...well...he will not be here. I mean — he will, but you will not see him."

"Just what I thought," cried the eldest. "Too proud to meet us. My dear, I think we had better go home."

"Yes, indeed!" said the second sister. "If your husband is too high and mighty to let himself be seen, then we are plainly not wanted here."

"Oh, no," said Psyche. "Please listen. You don't understand."

"We certainly do not."

And poor Psyche, unable to bear her sisters' cruel words, told them how things were. The two sisters sat at the table, listening. They were so fascinated they even forgot to eat, which was unusual for them.

"Oh, my heavens!" cried the eldest. "It's worse than I thought."

"Much, much worse," said the second. "The oracle was right. You *have* married a monster."

"Oh, no, no," cried Psyche. "Not a monster! But the most beautiful creature in the world!"

"Beautiful creatures like to be seen," said the eldest. "It is the nature of beauty to be seen. Only ugliness hides itself away. You have married a monster."

"A monster," said the second. "Yes, a monster — a dragon — some scaly creature with many heads that devours young maidens once they're fattened. No wonder he feeds you so well."

"That's it!" said the elder. "He's trying to fatten you up. You'd better eat lightly."

"Poor child — how can we save her?"

"We cannot save her. He's too powerful, this monster. She must save herself."

"I won't listen to another word!" cried Psyche, leaping up. "You are wicked, evil-minded shrews, both of you! I'm ashamed of you. Ashamed of myself for listening to you. I never want to see you again. Never!"

Psyche struck a gong and the table was snatched away. A window flew open and the West Wind swept in. He curled his arms about the two sisters and swept them out of the castle and back to their own homes. Psyche was left alone, frightened, bitterly unhappy, longing for her husband. But there were still many hours till nightfall. All that long hideous afternoon she brooded over what her sisters had said. The words stuck in her mind like poison thorns. They festered in her head, throwing her into a fever of doubt.

She knew that her husband was good. She knew he was beautiful. But still — why didn't he let her see him? What did he do during the day?

Other words of her sisters came back to her: "How do you know what he does when he's not here? Perhaps he has a dozen castles scattered about the countryside, a bride in each one. Perhaps he visits them all."

Then jealousy, more terrible than fear, began to gnaw at Psyche. She was not really afraid that her husband was a monster. Nor was she at all afraid of being devoured. If he did not love her, she wanted to die anyway. But the idea that he might have other brides, other castles, clawed at her. It sent her almost mad. She knew she had to settle her doubts once and for all.

So as soon as dusk began to fill the room, she took a lamp, trimmed the wick, and poured in the oil. Then she lit the lamp, and hid it in a niche of the wall, where its light could not be seen.

Late that night, when her husband had fallen asleep, Psyche crept out of bed and took the lamp out of its hiding place. She tiptoed back to where he slept and held the light over him. There in the dim wavering glow she saw a god sleeping. It was Cupid himself, the archer of love, youngest and most beautiful of the gods. He wore a quiver of golden darts even as he slept. Her heart sang at the sight of his beauty. She leaned over to kiss his face, still holding the lamp, and a drop of hot oil fell on his bare shoulder.

He started up and seized the lamp, dousing its light. Psyche reached for him, but she felt him push her away. She heard his voice saying:

"Wretched girl, you are not ready to accept love. Yes, I am love itself, and I cannot live where I am not trusted. Farewell, Psyche."

The voice was gone. Psyche rushed into the courtyard, calling after him, calling, "Husband! Husband!" She heard a dry crackling sound, and when she looked back the castle was gone too. The courtyard was gone. Everything was gone. Psyche stood among weeds and brambles. All the good things that had belonged to her had vanished with her love.

From that night on, she roamed the woods, searching. And some say she still searches the woods and the dark places. Some say that Venus, the goddess of love, turned her into an owl who sees best in the dark, and cries, "Who...? Who...?"

Others say she was turned into a bat that haunts old ruins and sees only by night.

Others say that Cupid forgave her, finally. That he came back for her, and took her up to Mount Olympus. It is Psyche's special task, they say, to undo the mischief done to a marriage by the families of the bride and groom. When they visit, and say, "This, this, this...that, that,

that...better look for yourself...seeing's believing, seeing's believing," then Psyche calls the West Wind who whisks the in-laws away — and she herself, invisible, whispers to the bride and groom that only those who love know the secret of love, that believing is seeing.

The Man
Who Overcame Death

Orpheus was a young poet with the most beautiful singing voice in the memory of man or god. He had been taught to play the lyre by Apollo, god of music, and there were those who said that the pupil played better than the teacher.

Orpheus wrote his own songs, both words and music. The fishermen used to coax him to go sailing with them, for the fish would come up from the depths of the sea to hear him. They would sit on their tails and listen to him play, and so they became easy for the fishermen to catch. But they were not always caught, for as soon as Orpheus began to play, the fishermen forgot all about their nets. They sat on deck and listened, their mouths open — just like the fish. And when Orpheus had finished, the fish dived, the fishermen awoke, and all was as before.

When Orpheus played in the fields, animals followed him — sheep and cows and goats. Not only the tame animals, but the wild ones too — the shy deer, and wolves and bears. They all followed him. They streamed across the fields, so busy listening that the bears and wolves did not think of eating the sheep until the music had stopped, and it was too late. Then they went off, growling to themselves about the chance they had missed.

The older he grew, the more beautifully Orpheus played. Soon not only animals but trees followed him as he walked. They wrenched themselves out of the earth and hobbled after him on their twisted roots. Where Orpheus played you can still see circles of trees that stood listening.

People followed him too, as he strolled about playing and singing. Men and women, boys and girls — especially girls. But as time passed and faces changed, Orpheus noticed that one face was always there. It was always there in front, listening when he played. The girl not only came to listen when he played for people, she also appeared among the animals and trees that followed him as he played. Finally he knew that wherever he might be, wherever he might strike up his lyre and raise his voice in song — whether among people, or animals, or trees and rocks — she would be there, very slender and still, with huge dark eyes and long black hair and a face like a rose.

One day Orpheus took her aside and spoke to her. Her name was Eurydice. She said she wanted to do nothing but be where he was, always. She said she knew she could not hope for him to love her, but that would not stop her from following him and serving him in any way she could.

Now this is the kind of thing any man likes to hear in any age, particularly a poet. And although Orpheus was admired by many women and could have had his choice, he decided that he must have Eurydice. And so he married her.

They lived happily, very happily, for a year and a day. They lived in a little house near the river in a grove of trees, and they were so happy that they rarely left home. People began to wonder why Orpheus was never seen about, why his wonderful lyre was never heard. They began to gossip, as people do. Some said Orpheus was dead, killed by the jealous Apollo for playing so well. Others said he had married a river nymph, and lived now at the bottom of the river, coming up only at dawn to blow tunes upon the reeds that grew thickly near the shore. Still others said that he had married dangerously, that he lived with a sorceress, who made herself so beautiful that Orpheus was chained to her side, and would not leave her even for a moment.

It was this last rumor that people chose to believe. Among them was a stranger, a young prince of Athens, who was a mighty hunter. The prince decided that he must see this beautiful enchantress, and stationed himself in a grove of trees to watch the house. At last he saw a girl come out of the house and make her way through the trees and down the path to the river. He followed. When he got close enough to see how beautiful she was, he hurtled toward her, crashing like a wild boar through the trees. Eurydice looked up, and saw a stranger charging toward her. Swiftly she ran toward the house, but she could hear the stranger close behind her. She doubled back toward the river and ran. Heedless of where she was going, she stepped full on a nest of coiled and sleeping snakes. They awoke immediately and bit her leg in so many places that she was dead before she fell. The prince, rushing up, found her lying in the reeds.

He left her body where he found it. There it lay until Orpheus, looking for her, came at dusk and saw her glimmering whitely like a fallen birch. By this time, Mercury had come and gone, taking her soul with him to the land of the dead, called Tartarus. Orpheus stood looking down at Eurydice. He did not weep. He touched a string of his lyre once, and it sobbed. He did not touch it again. He kept looking at his dead wife. She was pale and thin, her hair was tangled, her legs streaked with mud. She seemed so childlike. She did not belong dead. He would have to correct this. He turned abruptly, and set off across the field.

He entered Tartarus, the place of the dead, at the nearest point, a secret cave in the mountains. Orpheus walked through a cold mist until he came to the River Styx. He saw a horde of ghosts waiting there to be ferried across. But he could not find Eurydice. The ferry came back and put out its plank. The ghosts went on board, each one reaching under his tongue for the penny to pay the fare. But the ferryman, huge and swarthy and scowling, stopped Orpheus when he tried to embark.

"Stand off!" he cried. "Only the dead go here."

Orpheus touched his lyre and began to sing about streams running in the sunlight, and how good the river smells in the morning when you are young, and about the sound of oars dipping.

The old ferryman felt himself carried back to

his youth — to the time before he had been taken by Hades and put to work on the black river. He was so lost in memory that the oar fell from his hand. He stood dazed, tears streaming down his face, and Orpheus took up the oar and rowed across.

The ghosts filed off the ferry and through the gates of death. Orpheus followed them until he heard a hideous growling. An enormous dog with three heads, each one uglier than the next, was stalking toward him, slavering and snarling. It was the savage three-headed dog, Cerberus, who guarded the gates.

Orpheus unslung his lyre and played a hunting song. In it could be heard the faint far yapping of happy young hounds finding a fresh trail — dogs with one graceful head in the middle where it should be. He sang of dogs that are free to run through the light and shade of the forest chasing stags and wolves, not forced to stand forever before dark gates barking at ghosts.

Cerberus lay down and closed his six eyes. He went to sleep and dreamed of the days when he had been a real dog, before he had been captured and changed into a monster and trained as a watchdog for the dead. Orpheus stepped over him, and went through the gates.

He walked through the Flowery Fields singing

and playing. The ghosts there twittered with glee. Then he came to the Place of Torment, where sinners are specially punished. He saw the ghost of a wicked king named Sisyphus who was forced to spend eternity trying to roll a huge stone up a hill. Each time, just as Sisyphus reached the top of the hill, the stone rolled back, and he had to start pushing it up the hill again. But when Sisyphus heard Orpheus singing, he stopped pushing the stone. And the stone itself, poised on the side of the hill, listened and did not fall back.

Orpheus saw the ghost of another wicked king, Tantalus, who was tormented by an awful thirst. He stood waist-deep in a pure cool stream of water, but every time he stooped to drink, the water shrank away from his lips. That was his punishment; always to thirst and never to drink. Now, as Orpheus played, Tantalus listened and stopped ducking his head at the water. The music quenched his thirst.

Orpheus passed through the Place of Torment to the Judgment Place. When the three great judges of the dead heard his music, they fell to dreaming about the time when they had been young princes. They remembered the land battles and the sea battles they had fought, the beautiful maidens they had known, and the flashing swords they had used. They remembered all the days gone by. They sat there listening to the music, their eyes blinded with tears, forgetting to pass judgment.

But Hades, king of the underworld, lord of the dead, knew that the work of his kingdom was being neglected. He waited sternly on his throne as Orpheus approached.

"No more cheap minstrel tricks!" he cried. "I am a god. My rages are not to be calmed nor my laws broken. No one comes to Tartarus without being sent for. No one has before, and no one will again when the story is told of the torments I have invented for you."

Orpheus touched his lyre, and sang a song that made Hades remember a green field and a grove of trees and a slender girl painting flowers. The light about her head was of that special clearness that the gods saw when the world had just begun.

Orpheus sang of how pleasing that girl looked as she played with the flowers. And how the birds overhead gossiped about this, and the moles underground too, until the word reached down to gloomy Tartarus, where Hades heard and went up to see for himself. Orpheus sang of death's king seeing the girl for the first time in a great wash of early sunlight, and how he felt when he saw that stalk-slender girl in her tunic and green shoes among the flowers. Orpheus sang of the love that Hades felt when he put his mighty arm about the girl's waist, and drank her tears, and knew that at last he had found his bride.

That girl, Persephone, was queen now, and she sat at Hades' side. She began to cry. Hades looked at her, and she leaned forward and whispered to him. The king then turned to Orpheus. He did not weep, but no one had ever seen his eyes so brilliant.

"Your song has moved my queen," he said. "Speak. What is it you wish?"

"My wife."

"What have we to do with your wife?"

"She is here. She was brought here today. Her name is Eurydice. I wish to take her back with me."

"It is impossible," said Hades. "Whoever comes here does not return."

"Not so, great Hades," said Orpheus. "The gods can do what is impossible. Give me my wife again, oh king, for I will not leave without her — not for all the torments on earth, or below."

Orpheus touched his lyre again. The Furies, hearing the music, flew in on their hooked wings, their brass claws tinkling like bells. They poised in the air above the throne. The terrible hags cooed like doves, saying, "Just this once, Hades. Let him have her. Let her go."

Hades stood up then, black-caped and towering. He looked down at Orpheus and said, "I leave the poetry contests and loud celebrations to my nephew Apollo. But I, yes, even I of such gloomy habit, can be touched by music like yours. Especially when I hear my dread servants plead your cause. The Furies haven't had a good word to say for anyone since the beginning of time.

"Hear me then, Orpheus. You may have your wife. She will be given into your care, and you will lead her out of Tartarus to the upper world. But if during your journey you look back just once — then my mercy is withdrawn and Eurydice will be taken from you again — and forever. Go!"

Orpheus bowed once to Hades, once to Persephone, and lifting his head, smiled a half-smile at the hovering Furies. Then he turned and walked away. Hades gestured and as Orpheus walked through the fields of Tartarus, Eurydice fell into step behind him. He did not see her. He thought she was there, he was sure she was there. He thought he could hear her footfall, but the black grass was thick. He could not be sure. He thought he recognized her breathing — that faint sipping of breath he had heard so many nights near his ear. But the air was full of the howls of the tormented, and he could not be sure.

But Hades had given his word. Orpheus had to believe. And so he pictured the girl behind him, following as he led. He walked steadily through the Flowery Fields toward the brass gates. The gates opened. The three-headed dog still slept in the middle of the road. Orpheus stepped over him. Surely he could hear her now, walking behind him. But he could not turn around to see, and he could not be sure because of the cry of vultures which hung in the air above the River Styx. Then on the gangplank of the ferry, he heard a footfall behind him. Surely...why, oh why, did she step so lightly? He had always loved her lightness, but now he wished she was more heavy-footed.

Orpheus went to the bow of the ferry and gazed ahead. He clenched his teeth, and tensed his neck until it became a thick halter of muscle so he could not turn his head. When he left the ferry on the other side of the river, he climbed toward the cave. The air was full of the roaring of the great waterfall that fell chasm-deep toward the River Styx. He could not hear her footsteps, and he could not hear her breathing. But he kept a picture of her in his mind, seeing her face grow more and more vivid with excitement as she neared the upper world. Finally Orpheus saw a blade of light cutting the gloom. He knew it was the sun falling through the narrow cave. And he knew that he had brought his wife back to earth.

But had he? How did he know she was there? Hades might have tricked him after all. No one can call the gods to judgment. Who can accuse them if they lie? And he was dealing with cruel Hades, who had murdered a great doctor for pulling a patient back from death. Hades, whose demon mind had designed the landscape of Tartarus, the bolts of those gates, and a savage three-headed dog. Could such a mind be turned to mercy by a few notes of music, a few tears? Would Hades, who made the water always shrink from the thirst of Tantalus, and who rolled the great stone back on Sisyphus, allow a girl to return to her husband just because the husband had asked? Had Eurydice been following him through the Flowery Fields, through the paths of Tartarus, through the gates, over the river? Had it been Eurydice or only the echo of his own longing? Had he been tricked into coming back without her? Was it all for nothing? Or was she there?

Swiftly Orpheus turned and looked back. She was there. Eurydice was there. He reached out to take her hand and draw her into the light. But her hand turned to smoke. The arm turned to smoke. Her body became mist, a spout of mist.

And her face melted. The last to go was her mouth with its smile of welcome. But it too melted. The bright vapor blew it away in the fresh current of air that blew through the cave from the upper world.

Afterword

The Romans conquered ancient Greece but were conquered in turn by Greek ideas, especially by the Greek religion. The Romans simply took over the Greek gods, gave them Latin names, and worshipped them as their own. No one worships the gods and goddesses of Mount Olympus today, but they live on in wonderful stories that have been told and retold for 3,000 years, stories that we call myths.

In the tales in this book, we have used the names of the gods and goddesses that are most often heard or are easiest to pronounce. Sometimes we use the Greek name, sometimes the Latin, or Roman, name.

Here is a list of the most important gods and goddesses with their Greek and Latin names, and their titles.

Greek	Roman	Title
Zeus	Jupiter	King of the gods
Hera	Juno	Queen of the gods
Poseidon	Neptune	God of the sea
Hades	Pluto	God of the underworld
Apollo	Apollo	The sun god, *also* god of music and medicine
Artemis	Diana	Goddess of the moon
Athena	Minerva	Goddess of wisdom
Aphrodite	Venus	Goddess of love and beauty
Eros	Cupid	God of love
Hermes	Mercury	The messenger god
Hephaestus	Vulcan	God of fire and metal
Ares	Mars	God of war
Persephone	Proserpine	Queen of the underworld
Demeter	Ceres	Goddess of agriculture
Hestia	Vesta	Goddess of hearth and home
Dionysus	Bacchus	The wine god